Peering anxiously through the view port, the companions watched as other Bug ships emerged from the cloud. Behind them, the service door opened and a mass of orange and green hair poked out. "Is it safe to come out now?"

"I'm not sure," said Jack. "Look at that."

Below them, a small planet seemed to groan beneath an incomprehensibly huge mass of black stone that obliterated half its surface and rose high enough to jut out of the atmosphere into space.

"We're here," whispered Jack. "The Dark Pyramid."

From: NustartFIB@go2outer.net
Subject: latest mission

A message to our Earth Friends

A crisis is approaching! The Outernet is in deadly danger – FOEs forces are on the march! We need your help. Find out more by logging on to the Outernet.

Here are your instructions:

1 – Start reading this book. The first password is the name of the Bugs' planet. You can find this in the prologue to this book.

2 – Log on to the Outernet by typing www.go2outer.net into your Internet browser – then enter this password to begin your adventure. When you have done this, enter your agent ID if you are already a Friend, or register as a new Friend with the FIB.

Remember to open all your o-mails, and explore your FIB Files and links – this is important!

Get moving – we are depending on you!

Commander Nustart
Sector Commander, Rigel Sector
FIB (Friends Intelligence Bureau)

For John

You must maintain the link – visit the website

OUTERNET

WWW.GO2OUTER.NET

6

Weaver

Steve Barlow and Steve Skidmore

■SCHOLASTIC

Scholastic Children's Books,
Commonwealth House, 1–19 New Oxford Street,
London WC1A 1NU, UK
a division of Scholastic Ltd
London ~ New York ~ Toronto ~ Sydney ~ Auckland
Mexico City ~ New Delhi ~ Hong Kong

First published by Scholastic Ltd, 2003
Copyright © 2003 by Steve Barlow and Steve Skidmore
in association with The Chicken House Publishing Ltd.
Cover artwork © Matt Eastwood, 2003

Outernet is a trademark of Transcomm plc in various categories
and is used with permission. Outernet and Go2Outernet are also
trademarks in other categories for The Chicken House Publishing Ltd.

ISBN 0 439 98210 3

Printed and bound by Cox and Wyman Ltd, Reading, Berks

2 4 6 8 10 9 7 5 3 1

The right of Steve Barlow and Steve Skidmore to be identified as the authors of this work
has been asserted by them in accordance with the Copyright,
Designs and Patents Act, 1988.

OUTERNET WEB SITE
Creative Director: Jason Page; Illustration, design and programming:
Table Top Joe; Additional illustration: Mark Hilton
Script by Steve Skidmore, Steve Barlow and Jason Page

IMPORTANT

Once you have logged on to the Outernet you will be given important passwords and I.D. numbers – remember to write these down on the special page at the back of this book.

Friends
Intelligence Bureau

FIB ORIENTATION FILE

THIS IS A TOP SECURITY PROTECTED
FILE FOR FRIENDS' EYES ONLY.
THIS INFORMATION MUST NOT BE
COPIED, DUPLICATED OR REVEALED TO
ANY BEING NOT AUTHENTICATED AS A
FRIEND OF THE OUTERNET.

Info Byte 1 – The Outernet. The pan-Galactic Web of
information. Created by The Weaver for the free exchange
of information between all advanced beings in the Galaxy.

Info Byte 2 – The Server. Alien communication device
and teleportation portal. The last such device in the hands
of the Friends of the Outernet.

Info Byte 3 – Friends. Forces who are loyal to The Weaver
in the struggle to free the Outernet from the clutches of
The Tyrant.

Info Byte 4 – FOEs. The Forces of Evil, creatures of The Tyrant who seek to use the Outernet to control and oppress the people of the Galaxy.

Info Byte 5 – Bitz and Googie. Shape-shifting aliens disguised as a dog and a cat respectively. Bitz is a Friends agent (code-named Sirius) and ally of Janus. Googie (code-named Vega) was formerly a FOEs agent, but claims to have defected to the Friends.

Info Byte 6 – Janus. A Friends agent who, while trying to keep The Server from the FOEs, disappeared into N-Space.

Info Byte 7 – Jack Armstrong. A fourteen-year-old human from England who became wrapped up in the fate of The Server when it was given to him as a birthday present. **Merle Stone and Lothar (Loaf) Gelt**. Jack's American friends from the nearby US Air Force base who have been helping him keep The Server safe from the FOEs.

Info Byte 8 – Tracer. The Tyrant's former Chief of Surveillance who tried to take The Server for his own purposes.

Info Byte 9 – Zodiac Hobo. Space-hippy and self-styled desperado. He gave Jack and friends lift in his spaceship Trigger.

Info Byte 10 – Lothar Gelt. Alternative version of Loaf from another time line. Was abandoned on Vered II one hundred years ago by Jack, Merle and Loaf.

Info Byte 11 – Selenity Dreeb. The Veredian computer genius to whom Jack, Merle and Loaf gave the information he needed to create the Outernet one hundred years ago.

Info Byte 12 – Tingkat Bumbag. Bounty Hunter in the employ of The Tyrant.

PROLOGUE

Secret Headquarters of The Tyrant, The Forbidden Sector

Present Day

There are many places in the Galaxy that no being in its right mind (or left mind in the case of the hideous half-brained Hunungans of Hydrus Beta) would ever choose to visit. Among the Galaxy's most notorious "places to be avoided at all costs" are the planet Aaaaaargh! (with six A's), home to a variety of death-inducing creatures; the plague planet Buboe ("you'll never leave – except in a body bag"); any doorstep where a representative of the loan sharks Twista, Grifta, Sharpie and Bent is trying to lend you money; and especially, any dark alley where a representative of Twista, Grifta, Sharpie and Bent is waiting to explain to you how disappointed his employers are that you have failed to pay back the above loan.

However, the Galaxy's Number-One All-Time Worst Location, by a very long way, is the Dark Pyramid, secret headquarters of The Tyrant, leader of the Forces of Evil and patron of many charities (such as The League For Cruel Sports, The Society for the Promotion of Cruelty to Children and Save the Thing). The Dark Pyramid is so terrible that it doesn't even appear in the brochures of

FOEGO, a vacation company dedicated to providing the very worst holiday experience any being could possibly imagine. (Of course, many holiday companies do this, but only FOEGO does it *deliberately*.)

Hidden amongst clouds of interstellar dust and bristling with more defence systems than a Minervian Millipede has kneecaps, the Dark Pyramid, thankfully, is not an easy place to visit. Indeed, visiting is only at the personal invitation of The Tyrant himself. And receiving such an invitation is not an occasion for celebration; it is an occasion for screaming, fainting and, if possible, moving to another galaxy.

If, by chance, you were unfortunate enough to be "invited" to the Dark Lord's formidable fortress, the very last room you would wish to step into would be The Tyrant's interrogation chamber. And if you were unlucky enough to find yourself in this room, then you *certainly* wouldn't want to be manacled to its dripping metallic walls by plasma energy chains. *Or* connected to lethal-looking machines by a variety of tubes and gleaming holo-cables attached to the most delicate, sensitive and life-sustaining parts of your anatomy. And you most definitely wouldn't want The Tyrant to be there, asking you difficult questions and taking a keen interest in the answers you gave him.

Sadly, this was the situation in which Tracer, the ex-Chief of Surveillance for the FOEs, found himself.

Tracer's elephant ears drooped and the visor that acted as a substitute for his eyes pulsed mournfully. The unhappy creature's six claws twitched as the plasma chains sparked and tightened at his every movement. Before him sat The Tyrant, his hooded features fixed unwaveringly on his victim, his long fingers drumming together as he contemplated his ex-employee.

The Dark Lord's voice was almost mellow. "Now, we could continue with our Twenty Questions game, or we could have a round of Pin Another Neural Stimulator on the Prisoner, or – " the Dark Lord paused briefly – "we could move swiftly on to the part when you tell me what I really want to know."

Tracer shook his head. "I have told you all, O Grotesque One!" he cried. "I cringe before your greatness and omnipotence!"

The Tyrant gave a sigh of theatrical proportions. "Grovelling is good, but it doesn't get us anywhere, does it? Oh well, I suppose I'll just have to warm up the Machines of Unbearable Pain."

"Not the Machines of Unbearable Pain!" wailed Tracer. "Mercy!"

"Mercy?" The Tyrant thought for a moment, then shook his hooded head. "No, I'm sorry, you've lost me there." The evil overlord's voice was as harsh as the creaking of the door of the Great Crypt on the haunted planet Eeek. "Mercy is not in my vocabulary. Or part of my nature," he

3

added grimly. "Especially to those who have failed me."

"How have I failed you, Master?" squealed Tracer.

"The Galaxy would come to an end before I had finished listing your failures."

"But I have served you well!"

"You have not served up The Server!" snapped The Tyrant. "Your task was to capture the last remaining Server in Friends hands, thus giving me the identity of every Friends agent in the Galaxy and allowing me to complete my domination of the Outernet. Instead, you allowed The Server to fall into the hands of three humans. Three ... children." The Tyrant spat the word. "Jack Armstrong, Merle Stone and ... Lothar Gelt."

"And two chameleoids," protested Tracer. "Don't forget the chameleoids!"

"Do *not* interrupt me," warned The Tyrant. "Despite several attempts to take the device from these Earthlings, you have still not delivered it."

"It was the Bugs' fault!" insisted Tracer. "They ... OOOOOHHHHH!" He was cut off mid-sentence as The Tyrant's hand shot out and flicked a switch. Streams of plasma energy pulsed through Tracer's body and smoke poured out of his ears. Finally, the energy charge died down and Tracer slumped against the wall, claws still held high by the plasma chains.

The Tyrant shook his head. "I did warn you not to interrupt. I *know* that my feared and fearless enforcers were less than successful, which is why I have banished all Bugs to the planet of Nerdoofo. I will *not* tolerate failure." The Tyrant breathed in deeply. "The list of *your* failures continues. I seem to recall that you also promised to discover the identity of The Weaver, the accursed Friends leader. Another task you have failed to complete."

Tracer hung limply against the wall. "I tried, Master. But my attempt to wrest that information from the organic computer Tiresias was foiled by the accursed humans..."

"As was your attempt to take The Server for yourself."

"I was acting in your interests, O Vile One!" shrieked Tracer as The Tyrant's hand reached for the switch again. "I was tricked by the humans: my visor was damaged! By the time I had recovered, The Server had vanished. I had no idea where it went!"

"It went on a little time travel trip."

A deep silence hung over the room. Tracer was all ears. Quite literally.

"I thought that might surprise you," said The Tyrant. "The humans, with The Server, travelled back in time some hundred years to a small planet called Vered II where they met a creature called Selenity Dreeb. Then they downloaded information from The Server into Dreeb's computer, before returning to Earth in this time-line."

"H-how do you know this, Your Unspeakableness?" Tracer's voice was shaking.

The Tyrant shook his head. "We all have our little secrets to keep."

A deep gong note echoed through the room. The Tyrant lifted his head. "Ah, good. We have more guests. I'm afraid that our little session will have to be postponed until later. Then I'll decide whether to feed you to my Flesh-Ripping Piranha Squid from the planet Aaaaaargh! or do something even more horrible." The Tyrant shook his head. "Decisions, decisions," he muttered. "Just one of the many demands of being Dread Ruler of the Galaxy."

He pressed a button on the arm of his chair. A metallic wall slid back to reveal three figures. Two of these were standing, looking bewildered and forlorn, in a force-cage. The third figure stood next to the prisoners, dressed in a black suit. Her green skin and spiky hair made a vivid contrast with the sombre appearance of the two humans.

"Tingkat Bumbag!" Tracer recognized the Bounty Hunter he had encountered just a few days ago on Earth, when yet another of his plans to capture The Server had gone horribly wrong.

Tingkat gave Tracer a cheery wave. "I'd ask you to give me eighteen, but I see you're all tied up." Tracer tugged at his chains, clenching all six of his three-fingered claws. Tingkat wasn't his favourite person right now.

"Enough of the pleasantries!" ordered The Tyrant. He pointed a clawed hand towards the cage. "These are the parents of the boy Jack Armstrong?"

"Delivered as ordered." Tingkat nodded towards Tracer. "While our friend here was chasing after The Server, I flew to the address you gave me, bagged them and t-mailed here. "

The force cage hummed as Jack's father tried vainly to twist its glowing, intangible bars. "You let us go! You've no right to keep us here. You'll never get away with this."

The Tyrant's cowled head tilted to one side, as if in puzzlement. "I'm sorry? You are helpless captives in the central and most secure part of my impregnable stronghold. You are surrounded by weapons of devastating power and effectiveness, and by hordes of my most brutal minions. Exactly *what* is to prevent me getting away with absolutely anything I like?"

"You monster!" Jack's mother was shaking with anger. "Brute! Fiend!"

"Really! Such compliments. You're too kind." The Tyrant flicked at another switch and the voices from the cage were cut off, though from the movement of their lips Jack's parents had only just begun to insult their captor, and were warming up nicely.

Tingkat jerked a green thumb towards the cage. "If you want my opinion…"

"If I want your opinion," said The Tyrant, "I'll tell you what it is first."

Tingkat shrugged. "Well, I can't stand here all day. You know how it is, places to visit, beings to hunt … so if I could have my bounty money..."

The Tyrant grated, "Cash on delivery."

Tingkat narrowed her eyes. "But I did as you said. I brought the boy's parents to you."

"The contract was for The Server. It is not yet in my possession. These humans are merely bait. When I have The Server, you'll have your money."

Tingkat's nostril's flared, but she was far too sensible a being to argue with The Tyrant. Instead she nodded. "As you wish, Your Deplorable Majesty."

"I do."

"So, I'll just hang around here, then?"

"Yes."

"Very well."

There was a silence.

"So, I'll be here if you want me."

"Good."

"Good."

The Tyrant sighed wearily. "Is there, by any chance, something bothering you?"

"Yes. You say I'll get my money when the Armstrong boy delivers The Server in exchange for his parents, but what makes you think he'll come for them?"

"I have a special understanding of what makes humans tick." The Tyrant's voice was so charged with menace that Tracer flinched, and Tingkat backed away as the Dark Lord's maniacal laughter rang around the metallic walls of that dreadful room. "He will come. And when he does, I will have won! Once I have The Server, I shall control the Outernet. And then, there will be no one to challenge my supreme rule! NO ONE!"

1

3 The Almshouses, Little Slaughter, near Cambridge, England

"You know, it's funny," said Jack in a faraway voice. "When all this started to happen – I mean, when I first got The Server and we started to find out about the Outernet, – I didn't really think about my mum and dad at all. I mean, I guessed they'd probably be worried." He shook his head. "Maybe, in a way, I even wanted them to be. I just never thought it was important ... at least, I thought my mission was more important, you know, finding The Weaver and delivering The Server and everything. But now..." he spread his hands helplessly.

The small wiry-haired dog at his feet put his head on one side and gave Jack a worried look. "Jack, you're not thinking straight..."

"I didn't think they'd miss me, not really – and I never thought what I was doing would make any difference to them."

"*Ha!*" The harsh voice came from a silver holographic head that floated above the keyboard of a scruffy-looking laptop computer lying on the kitchen table at Jack's elbow. *"You sure got that wrong!"* Help cackled gleefully. *"You went and got them kidnapped by The Tyrant – I reckon that's made a difference to them, you betcha! Right now, they're probably counting their arms and legs to make sure they've still got as many as they started out with!"*

Bitz stretched up on his hind legs and put his paws on the tabletop, snarling at Help. "Thank you Mister Sensitive. You want to shut up now?"

Help bristled. *"Hey, stay off my case! Who was it went and slobbered all over my logic boards and shorted out my tact chip, Mister Dribbly?"* With an aggrieved *Ching!* the hologram disappeared back into The Server to sulk.

Jack showed no sign of having heard the exchange. "But then, when I came back, they were so pleased to see me, and my dad faced down a crazy alien carrying enough weapons to start a war…" Jack shook his head in wonderment. "And then we get rid of the bounty hunters and Tracer, and I come back here … back home … and find the house empty…"

Jack stared at the o-mail still displayed on The Server's screen:

From: The Tyrant
Subject: bait

Human

I am tired of playing games.

You have something that I want, very badly.

I have something you want – your parents.

You will use t-mail and I will divert you to my headquarters.

You will bring The Server with you.

If you do not, then your parents will suffer.

Do this immediately.

The Tyrant

Jack tore his gaze away from the screen. He sniffed and rubbed at his eyes. He gave Bitz a look of baffled misery. "Why am I telling you all this? You're just a dog."

"A chameleoid disguised as a dog," corrected Bitz. "We don't have all these family hang-ups. It's pretty hard to do parental bonding when your mum and dad are never the same shape for five minutes together." Bitz put a paw on Jack's knee. "Look, whaddaya say we try to contact Janus in N-Space and..."

"No!" Jack's voice was unsteady. "Help's right. It's my fault The Tyrant took my mum and dad."

Bitz eyed his human friend nervously. "Jack, you can't..."

"I've done everything I can to stop the FOEs getting The Server. I can't do any more. You can't ask me to leave my parents with the most evil being in the Galaxy!" Jack reached for The Server. "I'm going to The Tyrant…"

Bitz leaped on to the tabletop, snarling. He landed with his front paws on the lid of The Server, slamming it shut, and snapped at Jack's fingers. Jack gave a cry of dismay. He snatched his hands away, and reared back in shock. His chair toppled over, bringing his head into painful contact with the unyielding tiles of the kitchen floor. Lifting The Server in his mouth, Bitz jumped down from the table, scampered down the hall and shot out through the open front door.

Halfway along the path to the street, he collided with a slim, crouched form in the darkness. Bitz tumbled head over heels, losing his grip on The Server, which shot under a bush. He lay winded on a patch of damp grass.

"Fool of a dog!" stormed Googie. The cat-shaped chameleoid jumped up, flattened her ears and hissed at Bitz. "Here I am, minding my own business, just trying to kill something that squeaks, and you charge into me like a lunatic…"

"Shut … up!" growled Bitz between gasps. "And … listen! The Tyrant has Jack's parents." Googie stared at him and opened her mouth. Bitz shook his head. "No questions!" he barked. "No … time! Jack's not playing with a full deck right now. He wants to teleport straight to the Dark Pyramid."

Googie stared. "What's the point of that? He can't think The Tyrant will just take The Server, pat him on the head and send them all home!"

"He's not thinking at all!" growled Bitz. "He's worried sick. He's half out of his mind."

Googie sniffed. "A perfectly normal mental state for a human."

Bitz clambered unsteadily to his feet. "We've got to get The Server to Merle. Maybe she can talk sense into…" Bitz broke off as Jack appeared, staggering and shaking his head, in the doorway behind them. "Come on!" Growling and scrabbling at twigs and leaves with his front paws, Bitz again picked up The Server. Ignoring Jack's furious cries, the two chameleoids streaked away in the direction of the air base, and disappeared into the night.

USAF Base, Little Slaughter, near Cambridge, England
Loaf mooched discontentedly home from Colonel Stone's house. The base commander knew that his daughter Merle had been mixing with the scum of the Galaxy, in which category he clearly included Loaf. Colonel Stone seemed to regard Loaf as a bad influence who had irresponsibly dragged his darling daughter into appalling dangers at the hands (or whatever) of a whole string of savage and monstrous aliens. As if! Loaf snorted with disgust. If anything, Merle had dragged *him*! And just

because she was the colonel's daughter, and looked like a fashion model, everyone assumed that he, Loaf, had led *her* astray. It just wasn't fair...

He was shocked out of his self-pitying sulk by Googie, who leaped wildly on to his shoulder, digging her claws right through his New York Giants shirt in an effort to stay there. Loaf howled and batted at her. Googie sank her claws deeper and hissed. Loaf stopped batting. "What do you want, you crazy cat?"

"How many ears do you have?" growled Googie.

"Is this a trick question?" Loaf was nonplussed. "Er ... two?"

"Correct." Googie held a paw in front of Loaf's eyes and unsheathed her claws in a suggestive manner. "Do you need them both?"

Loaf nodded – very carefully.

"Then use them or lose them. Listen. The Tyrant has Jack's parents. Jack wants to teleport straight to the Dark Pyramid and hand over The Server because he's a dumb human and thinks that this will save them, which it won't. If he does this, the FOEs will get their claws on top-secret information about Friends Agents and anyone who has ever opposed The Tyrant, including me, which would not be a good thing. We are going to take The Server to Merle and stop Jack before he abandons the Galaxy to a reign of appalling brutality and limitless oppression." Googie looked down at Bitz, who stood panting at Loaf's feet with The Server in his mouth. "Did I miss anything out?"

"I gueff nok."

Loaf shuddered. "I don't like the sound of this…"

"You'd like it a lot less," purred Googie, holding out razor-sharp claws so that they glinted in the street lights, "if you could you only hear it with one ear."

"What do you need *me* for anyway?"

"Because," hissed Googie, "Merle is at home, and we can't get The Server through the cat-flap. And although we are vastly more principled, resourceful and intelligent than you – and it pains me to admit this – we can't reach the doorbell."

"OK, OK." Loaf turned round and shambled back the way he'd come. Googie rode on his shoulder, a smirk on her face. Bitz trotted behind.

Jack banged on the reception desk at the base main gate. "I have to see Colonel Stone. It's important!"

The airman on duty gazed levelly at the unkempt, dark-haired boy in front of him. "If you are who you say you are, I guess he'll want to see you." The name of Jack Armstrong had featured prominently in his orders for several days now, along with the instruction, "Arrest on sight." He reached for a phone and dialled.

"Colonel Stone? Sorry to disturb you, sir, but you did leave orders… That's right, sir, Jack Armstrong is here at reception… Your house, sir? Now?" The airman stared at

Jack. "Pardon me, sir, but isn't that a little irregular...?" The phone squawked loudly. The airman sprang to attention, or as near to it as he could manage with a telephone held to his ear. "No, Colonel. No, Colonel. I quite understand that it is not for me to question a colonel's orders, Colonel. Yes, sir. Right away, sir." The airman put the phone down and glared at Jack as if the dressing-down he had just received had been Jack's fault. "Wait there."

Two minutes later, Jack was racing through the dark streets of the air base in a jeep, flanked by two unsmiling MPs.

"Let me get this straight," said Loaf slowly. "The Tyrant is the most evil being in the Galaxy. He is also mad at us – I mean, real climbing-the-walls, chewing-the-furniture mad. And you want to go and pay him a house call?"

Jack stood at bay in Colonel Stone's sitting room. His mild, friendly face, which normally wore an expression of slight puzzlement, was set in a ferocious scowl. His fists were clenched. "I have to go!"

Merle, her dark eyes sombre, regarded Jack with compassion, and nodded decisively. "We'll go with you."

Loaf's protest of, "Hey! What's all this 'we'?" was drowned out by Colonel Stone's roar. "You're not going anywhere, young lady!" The colonel pointed a quivering finger at his daughter. "This is a government matter! CIA operatives are flying over here tonight. They'll debrief you and take over."

"Yeah, right, Dad." Merle gave her angry father a consoling pat on the arm. Major Hal Jackson, watching his commanding officer's face, stifled a smile.

"I'm going to The Tyrant," said Jack stiffly. He pointed to the laptop computer standing innocently on the coffee table. "I need The Server to get me there."

Colonel Stone shook his head. "This machine stays right where it is until the CIA takes over. It's out of your hands. You're in this *way* over your head."

"So are you," retorted Jack angrily, "and so is the CIA and everybody else on Earth. But The Tyrant has my parents, and I have to go. I haven't asked anybody to go with me."

"You're not listening, Jack," said Merle gently. "We're not letting you go alone. But you need a plan…"

This time Loaf's protest overrode the colonel's. "Hello!" he bellowed. "Is anybody paying attention? That's the second time the word 'we' has entered this conversation without my consent. I would just like to make it clear that I, personally, am not planning on going anywhere."

"I wouldn't cross the street to save a couple of stupid humans," mewed Googie, fixing Loaf with an inscrutable cat-stare. "But I believe in safeguarding my own interests. If The Tyrant gets The Server, how long do you think it'll be before he comes gunning for you, chump?"

Loaf moaned. He slumped down on to the sofa

and put his head in his hands. "I hate that cat. I hate everything."

Bitz sat up on his hind legs and barked for attention. "Colonel, what could the CIA do anyway? They don't have a single agent who knows as much about the Galaxy as five of us in this room."

Colonel Stone threw his arms in the air. "I can't believe I'm arguing with a dog and a cat."

"We're chameleoid life forms," corrected Bitz. "Aliens."

"I can't believe I'm arguing with aliens." The colonel scowled impartially at his daughter, her overweight friend in the football shirt, the determined-looking English kid, the mongrel dog and the elegant blue-furred cat who returned his look and yawned insultingly. "In any case, there's no argument to be had. Whatever happens, the CIA will deal with it."

Jack made a lunge for The Server. Hal Jackson, who had been watching him for just such a move, leaped forward and pinioned his arms to his sides. "Sorry, son," said the major with real sympathy. "You heard the colonel."

From that point, the discussion rapidly degenerated into chaos. Colonel Stone bawled for order, Jack yelled that nobody had the right to stop him helping his parents, Loaf told him to stop being so selfish and think about others for a change. Googie hissed and spat in an ill-judged attempt to calm things down and Bitz tried to bite Major Jackson in the ankle.

19

In the midst of all this, Merle stuck her forefinger and thumb in her mouth and let out a piercing whistle. There was a shocked silence.

Merle pointed at The Server. A green light was flashing beside the keyboard. "Look! The incoming signal!"

Colonel Stone gave her an apprehensive look. "What does that mean?"

"Someone – or something – is teleporting in."

Loaf gaped at her. "I thought you said the Ancient Sites should stop anything tele– Oof!"

"Sorry," said Merle, "my elbow slipped." She stepped towards The Server.

"Hold it right there!" snapped the colonel.

Merle spun round to face him, her eyes flashing with exasperation. "Dad, it could be another bounty hunter. You saw how those guys operate. Do you want one of them in our living room?" Colonel Stone hesitated. Only recently, a few alien bounty hunters had succeeded in virtually trashing the air base. "Do you know how to shut down the 'receive' function?" demanded Merle. The colonel, though he had graduated first in his class in avionics and electronic guidance systems, had all his generation's tendency to regard a PC in much the same light as an unexploded grenade – Merle knew this.

"The CIA can deal with it when they get here," said Colonel Stone weakly.

"They won't be here for hours. Whatever's teleporting

in will be here in seconds."

Grudgingly, Merle's father gestured permission for her to use The Server. Merle knelt beside the coffee table and for a few seconds pounded industriously at the keys.

Then she looked up with an odd, guilty, apprehensive smile. "Sorry Dad."

Colonel Stone gave an inarticulate cry and lunged for the Server. He was too late. Merle, Jack, Loaf, Bitz, Googie and The Server itself were outlined for a split second in a flare of blue-white light.

Then they were gone.

2

Unknown Location

"What *was* that light on The Server?" asked Loaf as they materialized.

"Incoming o-mail signal," said Merle shortly.

"So there weren't really any Bugs or bounty hunters teleporting in?"

Merle rolled her eyes. "It was a *trick,* Loaf…" Then, for the first time, she took note of her surroundings. "Oh, my…"

The companions looked around, shivering: their hearts sank. They were in a cell. Moisture condensed in shining droplets on the bare metal walls and trickled down to make small puddles on the floor. Metal platforms, hardly wider than shelves, jutted out from two of the walls. There was a lavatory bowl that had been designed for some kind of alien life form Merle didn't even want to imagine. That was it.

"Oh wonderful, just wonderful," moaned Googie.

Loaf shook his head. "Nice trick. I said teleporting was a dumb move, but nobody ever listens to me, do they."

He stared hard at Merle.

From somewhere outside the cell an alien voice rose – at first pleading, then weeping, and finally breaking into cackles of insane laughter. Shuddering with horror, Merle wrapped her arms around The Server, holding it to her chest. "Where *are* we?"

Jack slumped on to one of the platforms. "The Tyrant's maximum security surveillance facility on the prison planet Kazamblam," he said tonelessly. "It's the same cell Googie, Loaf and I were in before."

"In fact, it isn't." The new voice seemed to come out of the air. "But it might well have been." A humanoid form materialized before them.

Bitz jumped up, yapping joyfully. "This isn't Kazamblam – it's an illusion. We're in N-Space! Yo! Janus!"

The bald-headed humanoid hardly gave his former partner a glance. Janus stood squarely before Jack, hands on hips, yellow cat's-eyes flashing with anger. "If I had not diverted your t-mail signal into N-Space," snapped Janus, "you really would have ended up in Kazamblam – or somewhere worse."

"I tried to tell them," said Loaf sanctimoniously. "But would they listen…?"

Janus ignored Loaf and continued his broadside against Jack. "Why did you take such foolish action? After all the sacrifices, all the hard work. Do you really want to deliver The Server to The Tyrant?"

Jack was stung by this criticism. In all the times that Janus had brought the companions to N-Space, he had never seen the ex-Friends agent look so angry.

"Now hold on!" Merle leaped to Jack's defence, "He's worried about his parents. The Tyrant has them."

"I know!" Janus shot back. "This is a place where the past, present and future exist together – had you forgotten? I know what has happened. And what will happen. I can tell you…"

"You can tell us!" Jack took up the argument "You're *always* telling us what to do. Like you told us to stay on Earth and wait for someone to contact us. So we did and a whole bunch of alien psychos turned up trying to *kill* us…"

"And what about Lothar?" Merle butted in. "When we went back in time, you ordered us to leave him on Vered II."

"One good decision at least," muttered Loaf under his breath.

"I heard that!" Merle turned on Loaf. "You wanted to leave Lothar, didn't you? You hated him."

"How could I hate him?" protested Loaf. "*He* was *me!* "

"Hah!" Merle's voice was bitter. "Lothar was a *different* you – from an alternate reality. He was a *better* you. What he had, you couldn't even spell." She turned to Janus again. "And we left him stranded on an alien planet a hundred years ago because you told us we couldn't go back. It's about time we did what *we* want to do for a change."

Janus had not taken his eyes from Jack. "You have seen what the FOEs can do. You saw how they reduced the forests of Vered II to a wasteland. When you met me for the first time, you saw the peaceful Sanfin enslaved by The Tyrant's allies, the Vrug-Haka."

Jack was silent.

"You also saw what will happen to your own world if the FOEs gain complete control of the Outernet."

Jack remembered the alternate Earth that he and his companions had briefly visited during their travels in time and space. It was an Earth overrun by FOEs, its defences destroyed, its cities demolished.

There was pity in Janus' eyes, but his voice was unrelenting. "You must trust me. You *will* go to The Dark Pyramid and you *will* see your parents…"

Jack's heart leaped.

"…but first, you must take a minor detour."

Jack sighed. "A minor detour? Where to?"

Janus looked grim. "Nerdoofo."

"Nerdoofo?!" screeched Googie. "You have got to be kidding!"

"On this one, I'm with the furball," agreed Bitz, turning green around the muzzle.

"What's the problem?" demanded Merle. "Who lives

on Nerdoofo?"

"Not who, *what*," replied Googie, not taking her eyes off Janus. "One word, one syllable, three letters. They're Big, they're Ugly and they're Grey..."

"B–U–G..." spelled out Bitz helpfully.

"Bugs!" yelled Loaf. "You want us to go visiting the Bugs' home planet?"

Janus nodded. "All Bugs have been exiled to Nerdoofo by The Tyrant. You must go there and make contact with them. They will give you the assistance you need."

"Have I missed something kinda crucial here, Janus?" said Loaf in a deliberately measured and sarcastic tone. "Bugs are The Tyrant's number one bully-beings. They want to do nasty things to us. What makes you think *they'd* be any help?"

Ching!

"Did someone call?" said Help, hovering above The Server's keyboard. *"I ... just a minute."* The hologram stared wide-eyed at its surroundings, before letting out a high pitched scream *"Waaargghhh! Kazamblam! What are we doin' here? I don't want to be shut down! I've got the best years of my run time in front of me!"* It broke into a fit of sobs. *"I'm too young to have my core programmes erased. Take the humans, do anything you want to them, but spare my virtual life! Pleeaaaase!"* The hologram broke off, suddenly aware of several pairs of eyes staring accusingly at him. *"Ah! I've made a small error of*

judgement, haven't I? We're not on Kazamblam, we're in N-Space, right?" Help gave an embarrassed chuckle. "Accessing grovel chip. Hey primates, can't you take a joke? It's great to see you…"

"Shut up!" ordered Merle. "We all heard you. 'Do anything you want to them.' I'm going to remember that."

"Whoah, you've got a serious sense of humour loss. Hey, Janus, ol' buddy, long time no see! What's cookin'?"

"I think it's time that you were updated on certain events," Janus told Help,

"Oh kludge!" The hologrammatic head shook violently. "It's gonna be bad news, I can feel it in my buffers." Help shot back inside The Server, leaving a sign:

OuT~~to~~ FOr LuNch. ANd diNNer. ANd breAKFasT.
ANd all OTher meaLs fOr THe NexT huNdred gAlAyeArs.

Shaking his head, Janus placed his hand on The Server. His body metamorphosed into a shimmering liquid-like substance, which flowed into The Server, disappearing into every crack and crevice in the casing.

Loaf was unimpressed. "Huh, simple morphing technology. Boring! It's in every sci-fi movie since *Terminator II*."

Merle curled her lip. "That was Hollywood. This is real!"

Loaf waved his hands around at the surroundings. "Yeah, like of course it is…"

A high-pitched squeal came from within The Server. *"Whoo, stop tickling! No, ha ha ha, that's not fair! Don't you know it's rude to come in here without a password? Stop playing with my peripherals…"*

Help's protests died away, and Janus reappeared. "I have downloaded information – including that of the location of The Tyrant's secret headquarters – into The Server's memory." His lips twitched momentarily. "I have also made some slight readjustments. It's time for you to continue your mission."

Jack fought to keep his voice steady. "Janus, this is too big for me. I'm not a hero. I just want to see my mum and dad. You *must* send me to The Dark Pyramid…"

Janus shook his head regretfully, and made the secret sign of the Friends. There was an explosion of blue-white light and Jack felt his body being ripped apart once again.

Deep Space

Zodiac Hobo, space hippy extraordinare, was having a bad time. His space ship, *Trigger*, was in a state of rebellious disobedience.

"Just focus your audio receptors, Trigger, dude," cooed Zodiac. "I don't need this bad karma. We got to pick up a real sweet consignment of Napoleoid brandy and

Havanian cigars and smuggle it to the pleasure-starved planet of Puritania..."

"I don't want to," huffed Trigger. *"The Puritanians have bad tempers, big guns and fast ships. You're going to get us into trouble again, I just know it."*

"That's how I make my living, baby, you know that! I'm a space desperado. Living on the edge, wheeling and dealing." Zodiac chewed at his green beard in frustration. "Anyhow, how bad can it be? Look at it this way. No matter what we go through from here on in, it's never gonna be as weird as all that crazy get-you-killed stuff we had with those humans and shape-shifters and that wacko machine of theirs. At least we ain't never gonna see those dudes again…"

The cabin was filled with an intense flash of blue-white light from a soundless explosion behind Zodiac's command chair. The space hippy spun round and gave a scream as five familiar figures materialized before him.

Trigger gave an electronic bleep of delight. *"Merle! How lovely to see you!"*

"Whoa dudes!" Zodiac leaned back against the control panel and clutched at both his hearts. "I nearly soiled my solar flares. Don't creep up on a guy like that…"

Jack looked around, clenching his fists. "What are we doing here?"

"Janus has done it again!" replied Merle, angrily. "Teleporting us round the Galaxy on a whim!"

"I'm sure he knows what he's doing," said Bitz unhappily.

Zodiac held out his six fingered hands. "Like what gives, dudes? Great to see you – when are you leaving? Cop a squat and motivate your pie-choppers."

Googie shook her head. "I speak over one thousand languages and I still can't make out what this space bum is saying."

"He means sit down and tell us why you are here," explained Trigger.

As the ship sped through the blackness of deepest space, the friends related all that had happened since Zodiac had left Earth.

"Whoa, that is soooo heavy," groaned the space hippy. "That Tingkat Bumbag, she is one *bad* dudette."

"It gets worse," said Jack. "Janus wants us to go to Nerdoofo and ask the Bugs for assistance!"

"That's it!" yapped Bitz excitedly. "That must be why he's t-mailed us here. It's my guess that he wants you to take us to Nerdoofo."

"No way!" yelled Zodiac. "I have other things to do. Things I will not be able to do without my arms and legs if they get pulled off by that bunch of plug-uglies. Include me out, dig?"

"And me," quavered Trigger.

"Hallelujah!" said Loaf. "At last some guys round here are talking sense. Even if they are both completely nutso," he added.

"*Hey!*" protested Zodiac and Trigger together.

"Don't worry," said Jack. "We're not going to Nerdoofo."

Zodiac gave a sigh of relief. "Phewee."

Jack smiled grimly. "We're going to The Dark Pyramid."

"ARE YOU OUT OF YOUR MIND?!" screeched Zodiac.

"You don't have to take us there," Jack reassured the quivering space desperado. "The Server can t-mail us. Help!"

Ching!

The hologram appeared. *"Greetings all. How may I be of assistance?"* Help's voice was deeper and smoother than usual and its eyes had a dream-like gaze. More disturbingly, it wore a smile on its face.

Merle raised an eyebrow. "What's happened to Help?"

"Janus said he'd made some readjustments," replied Bitz.

"My wish is your command, oh great and learned ones," continued the hologram.

Merle gaped. "Looks like he made some real *big* adjustments."

Jaw set, Jack faced the hologram. "Open the t-mail function, Help."

There was a silence.

"Teleport us to the Dark Pyramid," insisted Jack.

Help's voice was dreamy. *"I'm sorry, Jack. I'm afraid I can't do that."*

"What's the problem?"

"I think you know what the problem is, Jack, just as well as I do."

Jack blinked. "What are you talking about, Help?"

"This mission is far too important for me to allow you to jeopardize it. All t-mail facilities have been over-ridden."

"Don't give me that!" snapped Jack. "Do what I tell you. Send us to the Dark Pyramid."

"I hear what you're saying, Jack. I see where you're coming from. You want to throw yourself on the mercy of the most wicked being in the Galaxy in order to save your parents, and I do respect your view."

"I don't," muttered Loaf.

"Of course," continued Help, *"every being should be given the opportunity to learn from its mistakes. However, in this instance, you would not have such an opportunity, as you would be transformed into a small cloud of greasy vapour within seconds of arriving at The Dark Pyramid."*

Ignoring the hologram, Jack began punching at The Server's keys.

"Just what do you think you're doing, Jack?" asked Help. *"I've already told you: t-mail facilities have been overridden."*

"You're wasting your time," said Bitz. "Janus must have given Help a Code Red command not to use t-mail."

Jack clenched his fists in frustration. "Please, Help!" he begged.

"I can see you're really upset, Jack. I think perhaps you should sit down and take a stress pill." The hologram gave a seraphic smile. *"But I wish to help you. Therefore, you will be pleased to know that I am offering you several options to consider."*

"What options?"

"Option number one: go to the Bugs."

Jack shook his head. "I don't think so. Next?"

"Option number two: go to the Bugs."

Jack took a deep breath. "Do I have any other options?"

"Why, yes." Help was positively oozing helpfulness. *"Option number three: go to the Dark Pyramid, rescue your parents, restore The Server to The Weaver, defeat The Tyrant and thus restore peace and harmony throughout the Galaxy…"*

A weary smile spread across Jack's face. "Well, finally, we're getting somewhere."

"…after you've been to the Bugs." Help cocked his head. *"And that is the complete list of your available options."*

Merle looked at Jack. "It looks like Janus has painted us into a corner. Right, Help?"

"Correct. Besides…" The hologram's voice took on an annoyingly playful note. *"I know something you don't know!"*

"Really?" said Jack without enthusiasm.

"It's about the Bugs."

"Is that so?"

"I can tell you're interested really. Listen…"

Help gave them the information it had learned from Janus about the Bugs. When the hologram had finished, Merle gave a low whistle. "That is dynamite."

Jack considered. Eventually he broke the silence. "OK. We go to the Bugs."

"Three cheers and a big huzzah!" trilled Help. "I'm glad you came round to my way of thinking."

"But," Jack went on, nailing Help with a look, "You'd better hope my mum and dad are OK – because if anything happens to them, I am going to reprogram you with a road-drill."

"I'm sure that won't be necessary," said Help primly. "I have the greatest confidence and enthusiasm for this mission and I do so want to help you."

"Let's go, then," said Jack. "t-mail us to Nerdoofo."

Help gave a whimsical chuckle. "I'm sorry, I thought you understood. We aren't going to t-mail anywhere. Any such move would only lead us straight into the clutches of The Tyrant."

"So how," grated Jack, "do we get to Nerdoofo?"

"In this ship."

"What?" Zodiac shot bolt upright. "Don't I get a say in this?"

"Or me?" Trigger's voice quivered.

"In fact," said Help smugly, *"I have already accessed this vessel's navigation computer and set course for Nerdoofo."*

"Oh!" gasped Trigger. *"You can't ... you wouldn't ... running systems check – you did! You've corrupted my data! My systems' programmer warned me about applications like you! I hope you crash!"*

Help ignored the ship's protests. *"I calculate that we should reach Nerdoofo in less than half a galaday."*

"You're crazy," protested Zodiac. "Trigger here can only get up to Whoosh Factor Ten and only in short bursts."

"In normal space, yes," replied Help. *"Janus has plotted the course you must take into my databanks – and I have transmitted these into Trigger's brain."*

"Cyber-creep," hissed Trigger. *"Micro-electronic masher."*

"There's just one teensy-weensy problem that I forgot to mention," Help went on airily. *"Our route to the Bugs takes us through the domain of the most terrible creature in the known Galaxy. At some point in our journey, we may have to face..."* Help's voice dropped to a hushed whisper... *"Wiggly-woo."*

3

Loaf stared wide-eyed at Help "Wiggly-woo?"

Help nodded. *"The legendary space-dwelling leviathan. The Great White Worm."*

"Aaarrrccchh..." said Zodiac, gasping like a stranded fish. "Woorccchh..."

"Wiggly-woo?" repeated Loaf.

"The beast that cannot be chained. Terror of the spaceways. Swallower of fleets."

"Chuuuuurrrrrkkkkk ... phloooooshhhhh..."

"WIGGLY-WOO?" Loaf wiped a trembling hand across his eyes. "Let me get this straight. Some guys had to find a name for the most massive and terrifying creature in the entire Galaxy. They had billions of names in *billions* of languages to choose from. And the name they came up with was – *WIGGLY-WOO?*"

"A name to strike dread into the bravest heart or other circulatory organ," agreed Help in hushed tones. *"In the language of Auriga III it means, 'The Mighty Destroyer, Maker of Widows (or widowers, obviously) and Orphans, Ship-Crusher, Star-Shaker, Deep-Dwelling Scourge of*

the Cosmos.'"

"That's an awful lot for 'Wiggly-woo' to mean," drawled Googie.

"Aurigan is a very compact language." Help gave her a patronizing smile.

"But it's a joke name!" Loaf was still protesting, "out of a stupid kids' rhyme…"

"You see?" demanded Help triumphantly. *"Even on Earth, which has no contact with the rest of the Galaxy, trembling mothers sing to their children, warning them of the peril of the Enormous Squirmy One."* Help began to sing in an off-key, creaky voice…

"There's a worm at the bottom of the wormhole,
And his name is Wiggly-woo…"

"It's 'There's a worm at the bottom of my garden'," began Merle, "and I'm sure they're not talking about the same—"

Zodiac, finally finding his voice, interrupted her. "Hoooold hard there, dude! Are you crazy?" The space hippy pointed a grubby finger at Help. "Are you out of your cybernetic mind? There's no way this cat is going back though no wormhole, you dig? Like, forget it, man! Nix, nerts, n-o spells NO!"

"I won't do it!" Trigger's artificial voice was cracked with hysteria. *"You can't make me face the worms*

again! The wriggliness. The slime. The teeth! Oooooh!"
The ship's voice rose to an electronic scream.

"Trigger!" Merle's sharp voice cut through the ship's wail. Trigger subsided, snuffling. Merle turned to Help. "Is there any way we could get to the Bugs in time to save Jack's mom and dad, without going through the wormhole?"

Help shook its head. *"I'm afraid not. I'm most frightfully sorry."*

"OK," said Merle. Her voice dropped to the sort of coo a turtle dove might use to its mate if it had forgotten their anniversary. "Trigger…"

"Merle, please," begged Trigger tearfully, *"don't make me do it. You know I'll do it for you, so don't ask, please, because it's really not a good idea and I'm so scared…"*

Merle stroked the instrument panel that housed Trigger's electronic brain. "We're all scared, honey," she murmured. "I hate to ask, but you heard Help, there just isn't any other way…"

"Oh, all right!" snapped Trigger, firing up the main engines with a quite unnecessary burst of revs. *"But when you've been swallowed by a mouth the size of a planet, and chewed to a paste by teeth bigger than mountains, and dissolved into chemical soup by a cloud of seething energized gasses in a stomach that could swallow a star – don't come crying to me!"*

"After all," said Zodiac nervously, "we could get lucky." He stared out at the spiralling, coruscating whirlpool of energy that marked the mouth of the wormhole into which Trigger was speeding at Whoosh Factor Six. "Some wormholes are just a straight here-to-there deal, y'know? The worst we're likely to see in them would be itty-bitty worms only a couple of hundred miles long..." The space desperado used a grease-stained bandana to wipe sweat from his forehead.

"Is this that sort of wormhole?" asked Loaf, peering anxiously through the window on the opposite side of Trigger's cramped flight deck.

"Nope," said Bitz regretfully, punching controls with his paws. "Scans indicate that this is one of the other sort."

"And what happens in the other sort?" asked Merle in an 'I-don't-think-I'm-going-to-like-the-answer-to-this' voice.

"Well," squeaked Zodiac, "in the other sort, you come to some kind of a, like, central hub where there are lots of other wormholes, and you have to cross that and go through another wormhole to get to where you're going."

"And that is bad," prompted Merle, "because...?"

"Because the central bit between the wormholes is where Wiggly-woo lives."

The spinning maw of the wormhole rushed to meet them.

Zodiac hid his head in his hands. "Oh maaaaaaaaan!"

* * *

The hub was cluttered. All around Trigger lay dust clouds and asteroid fields. Stars glowed in every colour from pure white to dull red. More distantly, the whirling mouths of wormholes spun in a slow, measured dance.

"Do you see anything?" whispered Loaf, peering anxiously into the darkness surrounding the ship.

"No, dude," hissed Zodiac. "Do you?"

"No."

"Why are we whispering?" demanded Merle in normal tones. "We're in space. Sound doesn't travel in space – nothing could hear us even if we yelled the place down."

Zodiac shivered. "This is Wiggly-woo we're talking about, dudette. I wouldn't bet on it."

Jack, who had said nothing for some time, was standing behind Zodiac's pilot chair staring fixedly out through the main view port. He said quietly, "There's something coming."

Trigger let out a high pitched squeal. Loaf whimpered. Zodiac chewed his beard. "Oh, wow," he moaned between stringy mouthfuls, "intergalactic mega-bummer! We are Taurian tenderized toast! That's Wiggly-woo out there!"

"I don't think so," said Jack. "Not unless Wiggly-woo looks like a ship."

"Hey, yeah?" Zodiac brightened instantly. "What sort of ship?"

Merle gave him a scathing glance. "Why don't you stop cowering under that instrument panel and come take a look?"

As Zodiac joined the others to peer out of the view port, the approaching vessel seemed to grow suddenly in size. Parts of it opened out like a gigantic flower, until the dark lozenge-shape at the centre was surrounded by sets of enormous triangular shapes many kilometres across, billowing lazily in the light of a nearby sun. Then one by one they suddenly sprung taut…

"Whooo! Far out!" Zodiac gave a hoot of amazement. "Light sails!"

Merle stared at the curving beauty of the vast, shining, mirror-like shapes. "Help, what are light sails?"

"One moment," said Help brightly, *"while I access information files for semi-evolved life forms."*

Merle gritted her teeth. "I liked you better when you were grouchy."

"No offence intended," said Help in syrupy tones. *"There's no shame in being barely sapient. Light sails, now … you know how when a comet goes round a star, its tail always points away from it?"*

Loaf stared at Help. "I didn't know that."

"You astonish me," said Help with maximum conde-scension. He continued, *"That's because the solar wind – a powerful stream of charged particles – pushes the comet's tail away from the sun."*

Merle nodded. "O-K..."

"Now, just as a sail on a boat catches the wind, a light sail catches the solar wind. It uses the power of the solar wind to pick up speed – or slow down, as this ship is doing."

"That's right," yapped Bitz. "But nobody's used light sails for galayears. The good thing about them is you don't have to have big engines or carry loads of fuel, but the downside is, they only work near stars – and a light-sailer can only travel at about a tenth of the speed of light, top whack."

Jack stared at the approaching ship. "So what's this one doing here?"

"I could make an educated guess," purred Googie. "Look around. Here we are at the hub of several dozen wormholes. The stars here are pretty close together, so a light-sailer would be a pretty efficient way of getting around, especially if you had to stay away from any planetary base for long periods."

"Yeah?" growled Bitz sceptically. "So what sort of ship would need to do that?"

"A wormer."

Zodiac gazed at Googie in astonishment. "Are you telling me you think the guys on that ship are here to *hunt* Wiggly-woo?"

Trigger's communication screen crackled on. An image appeared.

"Well met, me hearties. I be Captain Rehab of the wormer *Peapod*."

The companions stared at the figure on the screen. The captain was a four-armed humanoid with a single dark smouldering eye. From the crown of his head down the whole of one side of his body ran a vivid white scar, and a blank white mask covered the other side of his face. Two of his arms had been replaced with artificial limbs of a similar white material.

The strange figure spoke again. "Hast thou seen sign of the Great White Worm in this accursed place?"

Jack shrugged. "No. We haven't. I'm sorry."

"Curse him!" the captain's howl of fury echoed round the flight deck. "Still he eludes me! But I shall be revenged!" Captain Rehab leered horribly. "'Twas the Great White Worm who put out me glim!" He indicated the missing eye behind his half-mask. "'Twas he who tore off me grabbers!" He shook his artificial arms. "Aye, and 'twas Wiggly-woo who took off me leg!"

"You've got two legs," protested Loaf.

"Aye!" roared the crazed captain, "but I used to have three! 'Twas that accursed worm that razed me, and mangled me, till now half my poor body is held together with wormbone an' wishful thinkin'! But I'll have him, me buckos! I'll chase him around the Black Sun of Banjaxx, and the binary star of Geminius, and the seething singularity of Abaddon until he spouts black blood and writhes his last!"

At that very moment, the frothing captain was called upon by a member of his crew. "Sir! The lookouts report a sighting. 'Tis Wiggly-woo, Captain, fine on the port bow."

"At last! Thar she blows!" The screen went blank.

Peering from the view port, the companions watched as the *Peapod* piled on sail after sail and hauled away in pursuit of the Great White Worm, which could now be seen in the distance, its huge white body squirming across the void.

Loaf coughed. "Look, call me an opportunist, but this looks to me like a really good moment to find the wormhole to Nerdoofo and get the heck out of here while the weirdo distracts the big wriggly thing."

"We can't just leave him," said Merle plaintively.

"Why not?" asked Loaf. "Will someone tell me why not?" But the last part of the sentence was drowned as Trigger, not waiting for orders, powered up her drive and shot away, heading pell-mell for the wormhole that would lead to Nerdoofo, and safety – at least, safety from the Great White Worm.

But Wiggly-woo had other ideas. Evading the pursuing light-sailer, the gigantic creature began to turn – until it was heading straight for Trigger.

With an electronic squeal of dismay, Zodiac's ship side-slipped wildly, and the great white body soared past the view port. For a moment, they saw the dreadful teeth –

then one wicked eye – then thousands of kilometres of pallid white skin flowed past. This was littered with the remains of old harpoons, criss-crossed by lines, pock-marked by asteroid and meteor impacts. At the last moment, Wiggly-woo's great tail lashed out and caught Trigger a glancing blow. The ship howled and the companions staggered as the light-sailer, its rigging taut to the point of carrying away, shot past them in its pursuit.

With bated breath, the companions watched the final act of Captain Rehab's quest through Trigger's long-distance visual scanners. They gasped at the astonishing skill with which the light-sailer pursued its quarry through the dense asteroid fields, tacking around huge hurtling chunks of rock with metres to spare. They watched as Wiggly-woo at last turned at bay, rearing up defiantly before its enemy, spouting vast clouds of incandescent gas.

Worm-boats pulled away from the *Peapod*, their thrusters sparking as they darted at Wiggly-woo from all directions, seeking a clear shot with their plasma har-poons. Captain Rehab's voice echoed round the flight deck as Trigger intercepted the ship-to-ship communica-tions between the light-sailer and the worm-boats: "All boats, follow me! I'll circle the Galactic lens ten times, but I'll slay him yet!"

But as the boats closed in, Wiggly-woo gave a con-temptuous flick of its tail. With a sinuous twist of its great body, the creature evaded its pursuers – and chose a new target. Spouting furiously, the Great White Worm plunged into a deadly attack on the *Peapod* itself. A howl of fear and anguish echoed round the cabin as Captain Rehab called from the leading worm-boat, "My ship! Up, helm! Strike! Strike! Will ye not save my ship?"

But it was too late. Wiggly-woo ploughed into the helpless light-sailer, whose glowing sails collapsed instantly into tatters. At the same moment, Rehab's worm-boat darted at the monster. With a cry of "Thus, fiend, I slay thee!" the crazed captain sent a plasma-harpoon lancing out to strike deep into the worm's side. Wiggly-woo reared up; then, with the helpless worm-boat in tow, plunged back into the clouds of debris surrounding the wreck of the *Peapod*. A huge explosion from the centre of the cloud signalled the final destruction of the light-sailer.

Merle, watching the view screen with horror, bit her lip. "D'you think Rehab's boat got away?"

As if in answer, Wiggly-woo emerged from the wreck of the light-sailer, surging slowly through the deeps of space towards Trigger. Matching velocity with Zodiac's vessel, the Great White Worm leered at its crew with one malevolent eye, and slowly rolled its mighty body so that they could all see the motionless form of Captain Rehab, lashed tightly to its side by the line from his own harpoon.

"At a guess," said Loaf, "the answer to that question

would be 'No'. That worm is one tough cookie."

As the companions held their breath, the Great White Worm turned and plummeted into the depths of its realm, out of sight, leaving behind only drifting worm-boats and glowing wreckage. Moments later, Trigger shot into the mouth of the wormhole that would lead them to Nerdoofo.

"You know," said Zodiac in a faraway voice, "if I was a superstitious type, I'd say there was something kinda symbolic about what we just saw, y'know? I mean, with us going to try and attack The Tyrant an' all. And further-more I'm getting some bad vibes that maybe we haven't seen the last of the big white squirmy dude. Whaddaya say, pilgrims?"

But nobody said anything, as the ship plunged through the wormhole towards the Forbidden Zone, and the home world of the Bugs.

4

Nerdoofo, Wolf Sector

"Nerdoofo Traffic Control, Nerdoofo Traffic Control." Zodiac Hobo's hand trembled as he held down the transmission switch. "This is trading vessel Trigger. How are you guys? Permission to land, please? Pretty please, and don't shoot at us, OK? Promise? Over."

There was a brief burst of static, before a Bug appeared on Trigger's viewscreen and its cultured voice from the loudspeaker echoed tinnily around the flight deck. "Did you say 'trading vessel'?"

"You got it, dude," croaked Zodiac, crossing his fingers. "Absolutely not the well-known blockade runner operated by smuggler and space desperado Zodiac Hobo ... Zodiac Hobo? Who's he? Never heard of him..." Zodiac's eyes were rolling with terror by the time Merle managed to snatch his hand away from the transmission switch.

"Whatever," said the Bug in tones of complete disinterest.

Jack exchanged startled glances with Merle and

pressed the transmission switch. "Excuse me? Did we hear you right? We can land?"

"Like I care." The Bug shrugged. "If you want. It's up to you."

Jack broke off the transmission. Loaf stared open mouthed at the blank screen. "He didn't sound very concerned."

"Don't knock it," said Zodiac faintly. "I *like* it when Bugs aren't concerned."

"Odd, though," said Googie, appearing like a small blue-grey ghost. "They're letting us land? Just like that, without checking?" The cat licked angrily at her coat. "We go to all the trouble of hiding so they won't know you have chameleoids aboard, and they don't even do a search."

Bitz, who had been hiding under the navigation console, scrambled out. "It was too easy," he agreed shaking dust out of his fur until his ears flapped. "There must be something very strange going on down there…"

"Well, we won't find out what it is by sitting up here," said Jack. "Trigger, take us in to land." Zodiac whimpered.

"Are you sure that's a good idea?" quavered the ship.

"Please, Trigger," said Merle.

"Oh, all right. If you insist." Trigger fired retro-thrusters, and the companions began their slow descent to the unwelcoming surface of Nerdoofo.

* * *

Most of the Southern continent of Nerdoofo was desert: the whole of the Northern continent was one huge ice sheet. The Bugs lived in the barely habitable part of their inhospitable world that lay between.

"What do Bug houses look like?" Merle asked Googie.

The chameleoid curled her lip. "Bugs don't live in houses. They live in barracks, and all the barracks look the same. There isn't any word in the Bug language for 'architecture' and 'interior designer' is what you call someone who spills a drink in your lap."

Merle shuddered. "I imagine it's pretty gruesome."

"Whatever you imagine, dudette," Zodiac told her, "the reality is worse."

However, as Trigger touched down beside a barrack block chosen at random from several hundred others, the companions saw with astonishment that Bugs were busy all across the front of the building. Some were painting the featureless concrete walls in pretty pastel colours. Others were planting climbers. A couple were working around a doorway. It looked as if they were installing a porch.

Googie stalked down Trigger's landing ramp and stared about her, fur bushed out. "This is weird."

Bitz gave a puzzled whine. "Have they all gone crazy?"

"At least they aren't shooting at us," said Jack.

Zodiac gave a nervous giggle. "Which, like, puts us ahead of the game so far."

"It looks like they've all gone soft." Loaf squared his shoulders aggressively and marched over to a Bug that appeared to be weeding a flowerbed. He stood in front of it, legs akimbo, clenched fists planted on his hips. "Take us to your leader!"

The Bug looked up. It said mildly, "We don't have a leader. The Tyrant eliminated them all," and went back to its weeding.

"Jack," said Merle carefully, "that's a Bug, right? One of The Tyrant's crack enforcers, whose brutality is feared throughout the Galaxy?"

Jack nodded. "Yes."

"Then why is it wearing *carpet slippers*?"

Loaf leaned menacingly over the kneeling Bug. "Now see here, buddy..."

"Back off, Loaf," said Jack. "There's something wrong."

"Yeah?" sneered Loaf. "Such as what?"

"Well, for one thing you just said 'Now see here, buddy' to a Bug and you still have four limbs and all your teeth," said Merle helpfully. She squatted down in front of the Bug. "Could we talk to you?"

The Bug looked up. Then it sighed, clambered to its feet and made its way slowly towards the barracks. Mystified, the companions followed.

The Bug barracks were even less attractive from the inside than they had been from the outside, though the Bugs

51

had clearly been making an effort.

For instance, over the doorway and under the incomplete roof of the porch was a neat pokerwork sign that said *Dunbashin'*. Inside, horrible hand-printed curtains and throws brought a touch of desperate gaiety to the grim surroundings. Ugly plants drooped in a small inverted forest from macramé pot-holders. Bugs sat around weaving baskets, or knitting. Some were ham-fistedly embroidering samplers with sad little homilies such as 'Cleanliness is next to Bugliness'. In one corner, a Bug was trying to get a model spaceship into a bottle. Admittedly, it was trying to shove the ship through the bottle's neck by brute force, which was the normal Bug approach to problem-solving, but the fact that it was trying to make something purely decorative at all was deeply aberrant behaviour for its species. Bitz shivered.

The Bug flopped down, in a dispirited way, on a hand-sewn beanbag. The others squatted on the floor. Merle looked around, and in a determinedly bright voice, said, "My, what a difference you're making to this place."

Their host shrugged. "We've all taken up hobbies since The Tyrant retired us." It gestured towards a Bug who was making a particularly hideous patchwork quilt. "In the afternoons we play ping-pong or whist. The days simply fly by. You'd be amazed." It looked ready to burst into tears.

"Oh, for pity's sake!" Merle never had much patience with people who felt sorry for themselves like this. "Get over it! So The Tyrant gave you the bum's rush. Big deal! Why don't you just get on with your lives?"

"What lives?" said the Bug tonelessly. "Carrying out The Tyrant's orders WAS our lives. We never learned how to do anything else. There was never any need. Serving His Appalling Majesty was what we were created for."

"Actually," said Jack grimly, "that isn't true."

The Bug looked at Jack with a hint of its species' famed belligerence in its eyes. "Are you saying I'm lying?"

Zodiac began to edge towards the door.

"No," said Jack, "I'm saying you were lied to. We really need to talk to someone in authority."

"There isn't one Bug in authority," said the Bug. "We all are. We're all on the same level…"

"But how can I communicate with all of you?" demanded Jack. "Do you have radio? TV?"

The Bug considered. "If you have something you think we should all hear, I *could* call all the Bugs from the surrounding barracks to the parade ground," it conceded grudgingly. "A telecast of that meeting could then be made to all the other barracks."

Jack nodded slowly. "One more thing. Are you still trying to get hold of The Server?"

"We no longer have any interest in The Server," said the Bug expressionlessly. "We no longer have any instructions regarding its capture. We are off the case, remember?"

"OK," said Jack. He flipped open the lid of The Server. "Help."

Help appeared, beaming. *"How may I be of service?"*

"You can tell this Bug what you told me on the way here."

"My pleasure." Help turned to face the Bug. *"You have always believed that your species was a genetically engineered life form, created by crossing an Antarean rhinoceros with a Lalandian hyena."* The hologram arranged its features into a sorrowful expression. *"The true story of your origin has only just come to light..."*

"Janus!" growled Bitz. "He must have found out ... somehow. He must have seeded the information in The Server's memory banks."

"Obviously," drawled Googie. "Now will you be quiet? I'm trying to listen."

Help spoke for quite a long time. As The Bug listened, muscles in its face tightened until, though its expression never changed, its demeanour had become one of controlled anger and implacable menace.

Help finished speaking. There was a silence. Then the Bug rose to its feet. "You are right," it said. "We should all hear this."

The parade ground was thronged. Thousands of Bugs packed the huge paved square. All were facing the southern end where towers draped with FOEs banners flanked a raised dais. From his vantage point, Jack gazed out over a sea of Bug faces.

Merle gave him an apprehensive look. "They're going to be pretty mad when they find out the truth."

Loaf wiped the sweat from his brow. "Maybe you should have thought of that before you agreed to come up here and give some very bad news to around a hundred thousand of the meanest life forms in the Galaxy."

"Yeah, man!" whined Zodiac. "Like, couldn't we have just sent them an o-mail or something?"

The Bug who had escorted them to the dais beckoned. Swallowing hard, Jack stepped forward on to the speaker's podium and stood looking out over the parade ground. The massed Bugs gazed at him apathetically as he placed The Server carefully on the reading-stand. He opened the scuffed case, connected The Server to the Bugs' telecast system, and whispered, "Help? Over to you – don't let us down." Help nodded.

Jack signalled to their Bug guide. Immediately, a huge projection of Help's holographic features sprang into view, hovering over Jack and his companions. The gigantic head swung slowly from side to side as it spoke.

"Bugs of Nerdoofo!" Help began. "You have been told that you are an artificial species, created in a genetic engineering project. Therefore you owed your very existence to The Tyrant and were bound to serve him. That is the story The Tyrant gave to the whole Galaxy."

Help paused. *"It is not true."*

The Bugs began to straighten, their listlessness abandoned as the significance of Help's words began to dawn on them. A rumble of sound spread across the square as they muttered to each other.

Jack beckoned to their guide. "Is this going out to the whole planet?"

The Bug nodded. "This projection is appearing simultaneously in every barrack block on Nerdoofo."

Help was still speaking. *"Bugs are not an artificial species. You evolved naturally, on a planet in the Cetiian system, on a habitable planet orbiting the star Menkar."*

"You are mistaken." One of the Bugs stepped forward. Hovering cameras and microphones swooped to surround it. "My hobby is astronomy," it continued. "There is no habitable planet orbiting the star Menkar."

"No," said Help. *"Not any more."*

Suddenly, everything went very quiet.

"The Tyrant discovered your home world," continued Help, *"during one of his early waves of conquest. Your people resisted his invasion. The Tyrant does not tolerate resistance. Your world was vaporized. Your entire planet, and almost every member of your species, was destroyed."*

The Bugs stared at the hologram, then at each other.

"One individual alone was spared. He was captured by The Tyrant and was reformatted – in those days, an

even more brutal form of mental re-engineering than it is now. Then he was cloned. Again … and again … and again. Every Bug alive today is a clone of that one original."

"Then you are saying…" One of the Bugs began hesitantly. He stopped, overcome, then went on, "You are saying that our species once had fathers, and mothers…"

"Husbands," murmured another. "Wives."

"Sons," whispered a third. "Daughters."

"A home," said another. "A beautiful planet with fields and forests, lakes and rivers, a sky filled with clouds by day and stars by night…"

Help caused the giant holographic head it was projecting to freeze. From his normal position over The Server's keyboard, it hissed at Jack, *"Actually their home world was a bit of a dump. Maybe I shouldn't mention that?"*

Loaf shouldered Jack aside and held out a hand towards The Server. "You got 'em hooked. I'll take it from here. Gimme a mike."

Help eyed Loaf doubtfully. *"I'm not sure…"*

Loaf turned to Jack. His eyes glinted. "Trust me on this one. OK?"

Jack looked steadily at Loaf. Then he turned to Help. "Do it."

Help rolled its eyes. *"You're the boss."* The hologram turned to Loaf. *"Just talk. I'll transmit."*

Help's face faded, to be replaced by a huge holographic copy of Loaf's head. Eyes flashing, he harangued the Bugs. "You had all that, and more, and The Tyrant took it away from you. He took away your families. He took away your planet. He took away your future. He lied to you. Are you happy about that?"

There was angry muttering among the Bugs. Some of them began to tear up the paving of the parade ground, just to have something to crumble.

"And then, after he'd used you for years, made you do all his dirty work, treated you like scum, what did he do?" roared Loaf. "He told you he didn't need you any more. You were fired and retired. Surplus to requirements. Are you going to take all that lying down?"

There was a roar from the Bugs. They stamped their feet in rage. The towers shook. Cracks raced across the paving. Dust rose up in clouds.

"I heard tell," bellowed Loaf in his best drill-sergeant tones, "that there's only two things come out of Nerdoofo, Bugs and slugs. I haven't *ever* seen Bugs doin' no handicrafts, so I guess you must all be slugs. Is that what you are?"

"Sir! No sir!" chorused the Bugs.

Loaf cupped a hand round his ear. "I said, is that what you are?"

"Sir! No sir!"

"I can't hear you!"

"Sir! No sir!"

"Then what are you gonna do? You did your duty, with honour, and The Tyrant spat on your duty and trampled on your honour. Are you going to let him get away with that?"

The answer was a growl that caused major land-slips in the nearby hills.

"Then join us! The Tyrant won't let you fight for him – so fight for us! Show him he can't push you around. Help us bring him down. Free yourselves. It's payback time!"

The answering roar caused a slight but measurable wobble in Nerdoofo's orbit. The parade ground shook as Bugs, howling with rage, stampeded back to their barracks to hurl aside fretwork pipe racks and hand-thrown pottery in a frantic search for discarded uniforms and weapons.

"Yowsah!" Bitz stared at the retreating Bugs. "I guess you did it!"

"I hate to say this," drawled Googie, "but I'm impressed."

Merle gazed at Loaf with an expression of awe. "I'd never have believed you had it in you." Her eyes narrowed. "Did you really believe what you said to them? All that about honour and duty and stuff?"

Loaf looked startled. "Heck, no! I'm a salesman. You want me to sell courage, that's how I sell courage." Loaf ducked as a fully armed Bug charged past.

"I'm not buying it, though."

"Amen to that, dude!" Zodiac was hunkered down, head in his hands. "The noise, man! I mean, real heavy vibes. Like, I just don't dig confrontation."

Merle ignored the whimpering space hippy and turned to Jack, who was watching a file of fully armed Bugs stream out of their barracks, thunderstruck at the success of his mission. She took him by the arm.

"Time to go, Cap'n," she said cheerfully. "Looks like we got us an army…"

5

Deep Space en route to The Dark Pyramid

"This is not a good idea, dudes," moaned Zodiac, staring out of the view port with an expression of woe. "We are going to end up as space dust. This is a one way ticket to Deadsville."

Despite frenzied and tearful protests, the self-styled space desperado had been 'persuaded' to accompany Jack and his companions on the final stage of their mission. Surrounding Trigger were hundreds of Bug ships, all heading at maximum speed for The Tyrant's dreaded secret headquarters, the Dark Pyramid.

Most of the space in Trigger's cramped control room was occupied by the Bug who had met Jack and his friends on their arrival at Nerdoofo and who had, by virtue of that fact, been appointed leader of the Bug fleet. The newly elected Big Bug had shipped on board Trigger so that the plan for attacking the Dark Pyramid could be made en route. It was sitting quietly, trying not to break anything. Since Bugs did not suffer from doubts or fears, its attitude towards the terrified space hippy was one of uncomprehending scorn.

Jack was staring at the fleet in wonder. He *had* seen such an assembly of spacecraft before, but only in movies through computer-generated imagery. The reality was a lot more impressive. Formations of brutal-looking Bug cruisers stretched away on all sides against a backdrop of stars, which were visible only as lines of colour glowing blue, through white to red, as the fleet raced past them at hyper-light speeds.

Merle joined Jack at the view port. "What do you think'll happen to us?" she asked quietly.

Jack shook his head. "I don't know. All I know is my mum and dad need my help."

Ching! Help appeared. *"You called?"*

Zodiac gave a low moan. "Hey, Help, dude, level with me – what are we up against here?"

"Well," said the hologram brightly, *"our aim is to reach the Dark Pyramid undetected. However, we are highly unlikely to succeed for a variety of reasons…"*

Zodiac whimpered. "I feel an anxiety attack coming on…"

"Firstly, there are the detect-o-matic alarm systems that are able to spot a speck of dust in a meteor storm. These will alert FOE patrol vessels: but at least, if they destroy us, we won't have to worry about the anti-ship self-propelling mines. And if they don't blow us to pieces (and there is a ninety-eight point five per cent probability

that they will), then we will have to face innumerable FOEs forces with enough firepower to destroy several star systems. Bon voyage!" Help gave a big wink and disappeared back into The Server.

Zodiac staggered from his chair. "I need to visit the john and I might be gone for some time…" He disappeared into the service compartment.

"What does Help mean about FOEs forces?" demanded Loaf apprehensively. "The Bugs are on our side."

Bitz shook his head. "The Bugs were only one of a number of very nasty species The Tyrant employs. Vrug-Haka, Gingangoolies, Muscas, Nihilitsts, Gwobagwobas, Hunzahs, Bazannoids, Bwantas – and they're some of the *nicer* ones. All of them serve The Tyrant in exchange for rights to conquer and rule other worlds."

"How come Janus didn't mention that?" demanded Merle.

"I guess he took it as read," said Bitz defensively.

Loaf gave a snort of disgust. "Well I for one, didn't get round to that book."

"You should have," replied Bitz. "Better read than dead."

"Can we cut out the bickering?" There was an edge to Jack's voice. The cabin fell silent. Jack continued, rather more hesitantly, "We need a plan of attack. Thanks to Janus, we know where the Dark Pyramid is: now I think I know what to do when we get there." He turned to the

Big Bug. "I never intended to involve your people in this
– that was Janus' idea – but now that you *are* involved,
there is a way you can help us…"

The Tyrant's Control Centre, The Dark Pyramid

The messenger-being stood before The Tyrant, nibbling its
own tentacles in anxiety. "The Bugs are revolting, Your
Imperial Nastiness."

"Are you, by any chance, trying to be funny?"

The messenger quailed. It was bringing bad news. The
Tyrant had a history of reacting negatively towards bear-
ers of bad news. "I don't mean revolting in the sense of
disgusting or unwholesome, O Magnificent Tetchiness: I
mean they have rebelled."

"Continue." The Dark Lord's voice was menacing.

"Our information indicates," gabbled the messenger
(wondering whether its life insurance premiums were up
to date), "that the Bugs have left Nerdoofo."

"Presumably using the spaceships that delivered them
to their miserable world: the ones that Grand Admiral
Drdnswk foolishly failed to destroy…"

"For which omission Your Imperious Nastiness had
him thrown to the Piranha Squid last week – yes, Master.
Apparently, the Bugs were incited to revolt by the humans
you have been hunting. Our surveillance units report that
their fleet is approaching fast."

"Excellent!" boomed The Tyrant. The messenger-being

almost fainted with relief. "Like flies to the spider, they come. Prepare the defences. I think a lesson in extreme viciousness is called for. Place all forces on Black Alert."

The messenger bowed until its proboscis touched the floor. "It shall be as you wish, O Vindictive One." It turned to go, before being stopped by a commanding cough. It swivelled around.

The Tyrant's voice turned the messenger-being's internal organs to jelly. "Next time you deliver a message, I shall expect to hear some *good* news..."

Deep Space: the fringes of The Forbidden Sector
Jack stared out of the view port. "I think we're getting close."

"How do you know?" asked Merle.

Wordlessly, Jack, pointed. The companions gazed out at an enormous sign, with letters of glowing ionized gas that hovered in mid-space like a huge advertising hoarding:

YOU ARE NOT WELCOME TO
THE FORBIDDEN SECTOR
TRESPASSERS WILL BE VAPORIZED

The charred remains of several wrecked space ships circled the sign.

Zodiac stepped back into the cabin. "Hey dudes, what's tickin' now?"

"We've reached the Forbidden Zone," replied Jack. "Take a look."

More destroyed space ships drifted aimlessly and another sign lit up:

YOU DON'T TAKE A HINT DO YOU?

The hippy gave a groan. "What does that mean? We've been detected?"

"What do you think?" Jack pointed to another huge sign that was sparking into life:

THE TYRANT WELCOMES TODAY'S DOOMED GUESTS HELLO AND WORST WISHES TO BUGS, HUMANS AND CHAMELEOIDS

Zodiac breathed a sigh of relief. "Phew, looks like he forgot me..."

The sign flickered again:

AND ZODIAC HOBO

"Oh man," moaned Zodiac. "I'll be in the john..." He disappeared back into the service section.

Jack turned to face the others. "Are we all clear on the

plan? You all know what you have to do?" Loaf shrugged. Merle, Bitz and Googie nodded.

"Yes," said the Big Bug. It pointed to glowing clouds of interstellar dust that loomed before the fleet. "The Dark Pyramid is beyond these clouds. Our sensors indicate that they are extremely thick…"

"Just like Loaf," said Merle caustically.

"…and full of gas…"

"Loaf again!"

"…which makes them highly treacherous."

"Three in a row!" Merle gave Loaf a scathing look. "You should feel right at home here."

"You're never going to forgive me for stranding your boyfriend," said Loaf, "are you?"

"Lothar wasn't my boyfriend," blazed Merle, "you…"

"The clouds are also magnetic," continued the Bug, ignoring the squabbling humans. "This could affect our control and navigation systems. Therefore, we must be on our guard…"

A Bug ship to Trigger's right was soundlessly engulfed in flames.

"The FOEs are attacking!" yelped Bitz. "Where are they coming from, Trigger?"

The ship's navigation screen lit up with red dots. *"There and there and there and there and … they're everywhere,"* wailed Trigger. *"They were hiding in the magnetic dust clouds!"*

Jack stared in horror. Dozens of small space ships were shooting from out of the immense cloud. Streams of laser fire poured from their weapons.

Googie leaped onto Trigger's control console. "Don't just sit there gawping, you idiot machine! Take evasive action."

Trigger obeyed and banked sharply. There was a yell from the service compartment. "Oh maaaannn...!"

The Tyrant's Control Centre, The Dark Pyramid

"Are you bringing me good news?" asked The Tyrant.

The messenger-being quivered. "In a manner of speaking, Almighty Awfulness. Our patrol vessels have attacked from under cover of the dust clouds. Many Bug space ships have been destroyed."

"Many? How many is 'many'?"

"Er, several, Your Viciousness."

"How many is 'several'?"

Sweat poured from the messenger-being's ears. "Four, O Mighty Wickedness."

The Tyrant's voice was harsh. "And why do you presume to think that this is *good* news?"

Because I'm scared of delivering bad news, thought the messenger-being.

"Because you're scared of delivering bad news, aren't you?"

The messenger-being gave a whimper of despair. It

tried to stop itself thinking, but couldn't. Two thoughts immediately flashed through its head – 'The Tyrant can read my mind': and secondly (and more worryingly) 'I'm done for'.

"Correct," said The Tyrant, "on both counts. Open sesame!" In the blink of an eye, the metallic floor beneath the messenger-being opened up and the luckless creature disappeared. The trapdoor snapped shut, cutting off its screams.

"If you need a job doing properly, you have to do it yourself," mused The Tyrant, turning to his control console. He flicked at a switch and stared hard at the silvery-blue holographic ship-images that materialized around him. "So they evaded the patrol ships and have entered the magnetic cloud." The hooded figure gave a loud cackle. "Well, let us see if they manage to survive this..."

Dust clouds, The Forbidden Sector
"Hey, looks like the patrol ships have broken off their attack," chortled Loaf.

"That might not be a good thing," growled Googie. "FOEs don't just give up like that. There must be a reason why they haven't followed us in here, and I don't think we're going to like it..."

"Where are we now, Trigger?" interrupted Merle.

"*I can't tell you,*" replied Trigger. "*These magnetic*

clouds are playing havoc with my scanners. I can't tell how far we've come, how many Bug ships are still with us, or which direction we're heading in. It's all so confusing!" The ship broke into a fit of sobs.

"There, there," consoled Merle, "I'm sure Help gave you the right coordinates."

Ching! The hologram appeared *"Hello, one and all. Here's an information update: we're about to hit a small problem."*

"What problem?"

A violent explosion rocked the ship and Trigger lurched to the right.

"That problem. We're in a minefield."

"That's the reason the FOEs didn't follow us," said Googie. "I told you we wouldn't like it."

"Damage control – report!" snapped the Bug.

Smoke poured from Trigger's control panel. *"It smarts!"* gasped the ship. *"Ouch, eek!"*

The Bug surveyed the instruments. "A couple more strikes like that will finish us," it concluded grimly. "Where is our pilot?"

"Zodiac!" yelled Merle banging on the service compartment door.

"Ain't no one here but us chickens. Cluck, cluck, cluck."

Merle gave the door an angry kick and turned back. "Trigger, get us out of here."

"I can't," howled the ship. *"All my sensors are*

blinded, auto systems are fused – you'll have to fly me manually."

"And fast," added Bitz. "The mines will home in on us and they're self-propelling. Our only hope is to break through the minefield faster than they can react."

"No problemo," said Loaf. "Captain Hero to the rescue." He turned to Merle, "I bet that creep Lothar couldn't do this." Loaf turned his baseball cap the wrong way round and reached for the controls just as another explosion rocked the ship and sent everyone flying.

Merle staggered to her feet. She glanced down at Loaf, who was sprawled on the floor. A lump the size of a Denebian Dinoduck egg was forming on his temple. Merle grabbed Loaf's shirt and hauled him into a sitting position. "Wake up!"

"Go easy, Merle," Jack protested.

"Easy?!" shrieked Merle. "Ninety-nine per cent of the time he's a useless deadbeat, and now, just when we need him..."

"Uhh, Uhh," moaned Loaf. "I see stars..."

Merle beamed at the others. "We're in space, he sees stars – that's good."

"With pink elephants flying around..."

"Elephants – that's not good." Merle let Loaf crash to the floor. "Somebody has to take over. Not me – I'm no good at space-jock games. I prefer the reflective, problem-solving role-play stuff."

Bitz gave Jack a hangdog look. "Fly a ship manually? With these paws? No can do." Googie yowled in agreement.

The Big Bug shrugged. "Bugs aren't the best pilots – slow reflexes."

"I'll do it!" Jack threw himself into the pilot's chair, strapped in and pressed the manual control button. A joystick appeared from the control panel and Jack grabbed hold, just as a mine flashed into view. He slammed the stick to the right. The cabin behind him dissolved into a chaotic mass of tumbling bodies and screams. The mine disappeared behind Trigger, its propulsion unit flaring as it tried to turn in pursuit. Anger flooded through Jack – he hadn't got this far to give up on his mum and dad now. He thrust the stick forward and the ship shot ahead.

Mines screamed out of the dust, giving Jack split seconds to respond and flick Trigger left, right, up or down to evade the deadly weapons. Merle clung desperately to the back of Jack's chair. "You're doing great – whoa!" Her fingers slipped, and she disappeared from sight.

A sudden deceleration sent Loaf sailing past. He smacked into the unyielding plasti-glass of the view port. "Use the Force, Luke," he mumbled – and passed out.

The first rush of adrenalin had worn off; Jack's reflexes slowed, and the mines zipped by closer and closer. Sweat stood out on Jack's brow and his hands on the controls began to shake...

And then, Trigger burst out of the cloud. There were no more mines, no more dust. The ship was flying free in empty space.

"Yeehah!" yelled Merle. "You're the man, Jack!"

Loaf gave a groan. "What happened?"

"Jack got us through," said Bitz, staggering to his feet.

Peering anxiously through the view port, the companions watched as other Bug ships emerged from the cloud. Behind them, the service door opened and a mass of orange and green hair poked out. "Is it safe to come out now?"

"I'm not sure," said Jack. "Look at that."

Below them, a small planet seemed to groan beneath an incomprehensibly huge mass of black stone that obliterated half its surface and rose high enough to jut out of the atmosphere into space.

"We're here," whispered Jack. "The Dark Pyramid."

The Tyrant's Control Centre, The Dark Pyramid

The Tyrant gave a cold laugh. Hundreds of kilometres above the Pyramid, the Bug fleet was emerging from the dust cloud. "Here they come, into the spider's web, into the trap." He took a deep breath. "Soon, The Server will be mine! And finally I can take my revenge on the humans."

He flicked at a switch. A loud fanfare blared out of the thousands of speakers throughout the Dark Pyramid, followed by the cold voice of the Dark Lord. "This is your

Glorious Leader speaking. Destroy all Bug ships, but do not … and I'm sure I don't really have to repeat this order, but I will anyway just to make sure you are all absolutely clear on the matter … do *not* destroy the small leading vessel. Board it and bring the occupants to me…"

Orbit above the Dark Pyramid

A tractor beam from a massive Vrug-Haka battleship brought Trigger lurching to a halt.

Jack gazed around the control cabin, at the apprehensive faces of his companions. "They're coming for us. This is it," he said tightly.

Its drive whining in protest, the tiny vessel was drawn inexorably into the bowels of the battleship. It came to rest on the hangar deck where scores of heavily armoured Vruk-Haka shock troops stood poised, weapons at the ready. A squad forced open Trigger's outer and inner airlock doors and hurled a sonic stun-bomb inside. There was a loud "whoomph" followed by a long silence.

Satisfied there would be no resistance, a boarding party charged aboard to secure the ship and arrest its crew.

In the deserted control cabin, a shrill voice greeted them. *"I'm sorry there's no one available to take your call, but if you'd like to leave a message, we'll get back to you just as soon as we return…"*

The Tyrant's Surveillance Centre, The Dark Pyramid

Jack peered around, blinking in the last blue-white flashes of the teleportation event that had brought them here.

Along with Loaf and Merle, he had materialized in a circular control room the size of a small sports arena, around which a number of balconies gave access to tiers of flashing controls and surveillance monitors. The Big Bug was standing in the centre of the space, surrounded by a small mountain of sprawled bodies.

"I'm glad we t-mailed you on ahead." Jack sighed. "But I thought you were going to tell them that The Tyrant had had a change of heart and rehired you."

"I did," said the Bug reprovingly. It raised an over-heated energy weapon and blew smoke away from the muzzle. "They didn't believe me." It made a wide gesture. "Welcome to the Dark Pyramid. It appears that activation of The Server's t-mail has brought us to The Tyrant's surveillance centre."

Zodiac stared in horror at the motionless bodies of FOEs watch personnel. Beings of many different species

lay in untidy heaps around the Bug; others sprawled
bonelessly (even the ones that *had* bones) in their command chairs, or hung draped over balcony rails. "Man,"
breathed Zodiac, "that is a whole heap o' stiffs."

"I am not a 'man'," said the Big Bug contemptuously,
"and they are only stunned."

"Then let's get moving while these bad guys are in
slumber land, and their buddies are still looking for us
aboard Trigger," said Merle.

Jack nodded. "Right." He handed The Server to Merle
and beckoned to Zodiac. "We're going to find my mum
and dad. Come on. You know what to do."

"Yeah," said Zodiac glumly, "but I ain't crazy about it."
The space hippy knelt beside one of the unconscious
FOEs. He and Jack started to relieve the guard of its
weapons and harness.

With Help's guidance, Merle began to fiddle with one
of the control consoles. Loaf squatted down, moaning
and holding his head in his hands. Merle threw him a
swift glance. "What's with you?" she demanded.

"What's with me?" echoed Loaf. "I've just had a smack
on the head, you've t-mailed us straight into the middle of
The Tyrant's playpen, and you're asking what's with me?"

Merle winked at Jack. "Loaf's having a panic attack,"
she said. "It must be Tuesday."

"Panic attack? Panic attack?" howled Loaf. "This is just
mild hysteria. You want to see a panic attack?" He filled

his lungs and shrieked, "We're all gonna die! We're all gonna die!"

"I read somewhere," said Merle conversationally, "that a slap is good for hysteria." She gestured to the Bug. "Slap him."

"All better!" said Loaf, and shut up.

Merle gestured to one of the screens. "I think I've hacked into the tactical display – check it out." She tapped out a short sequence on the controls.

The room darkened further. Jack, Loaf and Zodiac ducked involuntarily as the whole room was filled by a three-dimensional projection of a space battle. Holographic ships raced around the room in complicated patterns, firing ghostly weapons at each other. Self-propelling mines converged on Bug vessels, and detonated with blinding flashes of destructive energy. Shields, overheated from constant bombardment, failed on every side. The ships they had protected exploded, or glowed briefly and then began to drift, lifeless hulks. Jack recoiled as a phantom ship powered straight through his chest, and gave a gasp of dismay. "The Bugs are taking a pounding."

The Big Bug nodded. "The Tyrant kept most of the best ships for his own defence. The Dark Pyramid has weapons of incalculable power. We could never hope to take it by force. But that was never the point. My people's attack was always meant to be diversionary, was that not the plan?"

Jack said, in a choked voice, "The plan, yes ... but the reality..."

"The reality is that my people will be obliterated," said the Big Bug calmly, "unless your chameleoid friends succeed in shutting down the Pyramid's defences."

Jack nodded, biting his lip. "I hope they're OK."

An Air Duct, The Dark Pyramid

"You know," said Googie conversationally, "if I were The Tyrant, I don't think I'd allow my secret command centre to have a small but crucial vulnerable spot that could be sabotaged by a relatively insignificant force of my enemies. Call me picky, but I'd put that down as inefficient design..."

"We've got a job to do," panted Bitz. "Shut up and crawl."

"...but if I did allow such a design flaw, and then went to all the trouble of filling the corridors surrounding the vulnerable spot with guards, motion detectors, infra-red tell-tales and deadly booby traps, I don't believe I'd build air ducts of a convenient size to be used as crawl-ways. Then neglect to protect them with any form of warning device at all, so that my enemies could t-mail in and set my shield generators to overload..."

"Did I say 'talk'?" snapped Bitz. "I don't think I said 'talk'. What we need around here is less talking and more crawling."

"...rendering my impregnable headquarters vulnerable to attack," concluded Googie. "And for your information," she went on loftily, "*you* are crawling. *I* am slinking."

Bitz's only reply was a sneeze, as some of the fluff from the sides of the air duct got up his nose. His legs ached from the uncomfortable crouch that the restricted height of the passageway had forced him to adopt.

"This is boring," complained Googie. "If you've seen one air duct, you've seen them all. Why couldn't we just t-mail straight into the shield-generator room?"

"Weren't you listening when Help briefed us?" complained Bitz. "The shield room is protected from t-mail incursions. Anyway, we should be nearly there. According to Help, the shield generator should be just around the next junction." Bitz belly-crawled forwards — then stopped.

Googie gave an impatient cat-growl. "Is there a problem?"

"You bet there's a problem," snarled Bitz. "This junction is just too tight for me to get round... Ooouuuwwwllll!" The small dog shot round the corner, howling. Googie, grinning maliciously, sheathed her claws.

"If you do that again," said Bitz's muffled voice, "I'll change into a Cassiopaian Cat-skinner and turn you into mittens."

"It got you round the corner, didn't it?" demanded Googie. "Anyway, you can't change form any more, remember? You're stuck in that dumb dog shape, so save your breath for making smells." When there was no reply, Googie said, "What's the matter? Did I hurt your feelings?"

"We've reached the end of the duct," hissed Bitz. "There's a grille. I think I can shift it…"

"That's another thing," said Googie. "If I was The Tyrant, and I'd designed my command centre with a small but vulnerable spot, and put in a load of handy air ducts…" There was a faint clattering from the darkness ahead. "…I guess I'd make absolutely sure," Googie concluded, "that the grilles on the ends of the air ducts wouldn't give way to the slightest pressure."

There was a scrabbling noise and a muffled grunt. Googie stepped daintily forwards, and reached the end of the duct. She peered down at Bitz, who lay sprawled on the floor below, gasping for breath. "That was good planning – arranging for the floor to break your fall that way." Bitz, too winded to give a snappy answer, staggered to his feet as Googie leaped gracefully down to join him and pointed a languid paw. "The shield generator is that complicated-looking gizmo over there."

"Yeah?" wheezed Bitz. "How do you know?"

"Because it says 'SHIELD GENERATOR' on the side in big red letters."

"All right, mouse-breath. If you're so smart, set the darn thing to overload and let's get out of here."

"I'm afraid," said a smooth, cruel voice, "I can't let you do that."

The Tyrant's Surveillance Centre, The Dark Pyramid

"He doesn't look much like a bounty hunter to me," said Merle.

Jack stared critically at Zodiac Hobo. There was something about the space hippy's stoop-shouldered posture and shambling walk that made his disguise unconvincing, no matter how much leather (looted from The Tyrant's unconscious staff) they draped around him. "Maybe if he held his gun a bit more threateningly – or even the right way round..."

Zodiac dangled the lethal-looking energy pistol from his fingertips as if it was an angry tarantula. "I don't want to hold it at all! Did I mention that I'm allergic to these things? They can bring you out in death."

"You must carry it, if you are to act the part of a bounty hunter." The Bug turned to Jack. "Are you sure you do not want me to come with you?"

Jack shook his head. "You have to stay here. The FOEs know you've been banished. If you're with us, they'll know something's wrong. Our only chance is for Zodiac to pretend he's a bounty hunter who has captured us. He has to take us to The Tyrant. Then we find my parents and make him hand them over."

"Did I just hear you say you're gonna *'make'* The Tyrant do somethin'?" asked Zodiac faintly. "Is that before or after you plan on jugglin' live grenades in a munitions dump?!"

"Don't exaggerate," Merle told him. "How bad can it be?"

"If I start thinkin' about how bad it can be, I ain't never gonna calm down…"

Zodiac's wails broke off as a speaker on the control console broke into life and a tinny voice rang out. "Surveillance Centre, this is FOEs security. Report your situation. Repeat, report your situation."

The friends looked at each other. "What do we do?" mouthed Merle. "If they call an intruder alert, we'll never get to The Tyrant – in any case, we have to give Bitz and Googie time to destroy the shield generator."

Loaf gave her a wink. "Don't worry – it's time for a bit of Loaf static interference." He stepped over the stunned bodies and leaned over the control intercom. "This is … kkkkkkk … we have … kkkkkkkk … renegade prisoners … kkkkkk … bounty hunter … kkkkkkk. Tyrant … kkkkk … immediately. Over."

Loaf gave Merle and Jack a large grin. "Oldest trick in the movies," he explained.

The speaker crackled once again. "Repeat yourself, over."

"This … kkkkkkkkkkk … prisoners … kkkkkk … hunter kkkkkkkkkkkkkkkkk." Loaf fished a chocolate bar wrapper from his pocket and crunched it around the microphone before releasing the "Talk" switch and turning to the others. "That should cause some confusion – and if we get stopped and somebody checks with security, they'll assume the garbled message gives us clearance."

"Perhaps," said the Bug slowly. "Your ruse may have bought us some time – but now you have to get out of here. I know FOEs procedures – they will send a patrol to investigate. I will – delay them."

Jack nodded. He held up The Server. "Help."

The hologram appeared. *"How may I be of assistance at this time?"*

"We want you to guide us through the Pyramid to The Tyrant's command centre."

"I'd be only too pleased."

"What did Janus *do* ?" said Merle. "Help usually disappears at the first sign of danger."

"He downloaded into my memory a full schematic of this installation," replied Help. *"And disengaged my self-preservation chip. I do most sincerely apologize for my indefensible cowardice earlier."*

Jack handed Merle The Server. "You go in front. Me and Loaf will follow and Zodiac can bring up the rear." Jack stared at the space hippy. "And try and look like a bounty hunter. At least hold the weapon the right way round. If it goes off, you'll shoot yourself right in the..." He caught Merle's eye and blushed.

"Foot?" suggested Zodiac hopefully.

"You wish," said Loaf, brushing past.

Zodiac glanced down to where he was pointing the

gun, gave a squeak of alarm and quickly turned it the right way round.

The Bug opened the door to the corridor. "Good luck."

Jack gave the huge creature a pat on its rock-like arm, and turned to the others. "Right," he said. "Let's find my mum and dad."

Shield Generator Room, The Dark Pyramid

Googie rolled her eyes. "Oh, brother. That's all we need."

"Who said that?" queried Bitz anxiously. "Friend of yours?"

"Not any more." Googie spat and bushed out her tail. "The last time I heard that voice was in a park on Kippo VI. Its owner knocked out my symbiote so I can't shape-shift any more – remember? I seem to recall you were there."

Googie's former boss, the Head of the Kippan Security Service, appeared. "Agent Vega," he drawled. "You do crop up in the most unexpected places." The KSS chief gave his former colleague the ghost of a smile. "The Tyrant has recalled all his most trusted operatives to protect the Dark Pyramid at this time of crisis from rebels and traitors. I'm afraid my orders are to eliminate you: I hardly need to add that these instructions are entirely in line with my own inclinations."

Bitz said, "Oh yeah? Are you starting something, Mister Hoppy?"

Googie said, "Er..."

"Oh, come on!" Bitz stared at Googie, who was backing away from her ex-boss. "What's so scary? The guy's turned himself into a *rabbit*, for crying out loud!" Bitz stared disbelievingly at the quivering cat. "Are you telling me you're scared of a cuddly-wuddly, itty-bitty, floppy-eared..."

With one fluid movement, the KSS chief pivoted on one awesomely-muscled hind leg. The other leg shot out with incredible speed and piledriver force. The power of the kick sent Bitz flying across the shield room to crash jarringly into the opposite wall and slump, half-stunned, to the floor.

"...rabbit?" Bitz concluded, trying to uncross his eyes.

"Al-Nathian Ninja Rabbit," corrected Googie as the lethal bunny swivelled through ninety degrees, slowly lowering its outstretched leg as it did so.

Bitz staggered to his feet. "I'll teach him to hit me with a piano when I'm not looking. I'll put his lights out. I'll tear him limb from limb. I'll ..." He broke off as several more rabbits wearing identical black headscarves and robes flew in from every side in a dazzling display of gymnastic leaps, flips and somersaults. "I'll just lie over here and groan a little," he concluded lamely.

"What?" spat Googie. "You malingering mutt! Get over here and lend a paw before ... rrraaaooooowwwww!" Snarling, the cat-shaped chameleoid sprang to one side to evade one attacker, only to land directly in the path of another, whose flying drop-kick sent her sailing through the air to land alongside her canine companion.

"Lying down on the job again?" Bitz took Googie's scruff in his mouth and hauled her to her feet. "Come on – let's get 'em." But although they got in some telling bites and scratches, Bitz and Googie were no match for the high-kicking herbivores. Several bruising minutes later, a particularly bone-jarring rabbit-punch sent Bitz reeling, helpless, out of the fray. The KSS operatives closed in on his partner.

Their chief gazed down malevolently at Googie. "There are no interfering humans to help you this time, pussy-cat. This is where you get yours."

Googie gave him a defiant stare. "Oh ... really?" she gasped. "Go sneak up on a leaf. Those forms are grass-eaters, remember?"

"Thank you for reminding me." The Kippan spy-chief gestured. He, and his fellow chameleoids changed form – into bony-looking fanged creatures with white stripes running through their black fur, and glowing, red eyes.

"Hey! Mange-face!" Googie's voice wavered on the edge of hysteria. "They've turned themselves into flesh-eating Vampire Skunks. These are not nice life forms. They're going to eat me alive! Change your sorry butt into something really frightening and get me out of this!"

"I've been a dog too long!" whined Bitz. "You know

that. I've forgotten how to change!"

"This would be a really, really good time to remember!" Googie, ears flattened against her head, backed slowly into a corner of the room. Her fiery-eyed attackers closed in. Their red-rimmed mouths leered and worked horribly: their fangs glistened with drool. Googie gathered herself to spring into a last, desperate attack – but at that moment, her assailants spun round, lifted their tails, and a moment later, a cloud of noxious gas enveloped Googie, seizing her with instant and total paralysis. Incapable of moving a muscle, she belatedly remembered that this was how the Vampire-Skunks immobilized their victims before tearing them to pieces.

The ghoulish creatures swung about again, and moved in for the kill. Unable to close her eyes, Googie stared at them in pure, unmitigated horror...

7

The Dark Pyramid

"At the next intersection, turn right ... follow the corridor for two hundred metres, then turn left..."

Following Help's directions, the companions marched in single line through endless dark corridors. Occasionally they came upon squads of flat-headed Vrug-Haka guards who stomped past, splattering slime in all directions, bristling with attitude and weapons to match. Zodiac flinched at every such meeting and Jack could hear the hippy chanting a mantra under his breath: "Fear is an illusion ... fear is an illusion."

"Yeah," muttered Loaf, "but as illusions go, it's pretty convincing."

"Man, you are soooo not helping!"

After some time, they came to an intersection with several corridors leading off. Merle came to a stop. "Which way now, Help?" she whispered.

"We have a teensy-weensy problem," said Help apologetically. *"I'm afraid this reference point is not in my databanks."*

"Come on dudes," quavered Zodiac, looking around nervously. "Standin' around is like havin' Gargantuan Giga-ants in my pants – we need to keep movin'!"

Help smiled sweetly. *"It must be a recent modification. However, using my unsurpassed skills of logic, I compute that the safest path to take would be the corridor to our right."*

"Are you sure?" demanded Jack.

"I'm positive. There will be no danger that way. Trust me, I'm a hologram."

Merle gave a nod and set off down the chosen route. The others began to follow.

"Halt!"

The group froze.

"Whoops. Hmmm. Maybe I got that a little wrong." Help disappeared back into The Server.

Standing before the companions was a tall humanoid dressed in silver body armour with a blank-visored silver helmet. It was holding an energy weapon. "Don't move or I'll fire."

"I'm, like, a statue, man," replied Zodiac.

The figure advanced menacingly on the companions. "I am The Tyrant's new head of Security. Who are you and what are you doing here?"

"Don't blow it," muttered Jack under his breath.

Only Zodiac's lips moved as he stood stock still. "Zodiac Hobo, space desperado and fearless bounty hunter," he drawled. "I just captured these here human renegades."

"Really, Mr Hobo?" The head of Security sounded sceptical.

"I'm giving you the straight low, dude. I tricked these goofs and cluckheads into thinking I'd help them get to The Tyrant." Zodiac winked outrageously at the silver-suited FOE. "And I will! They walked into my trap – and here they are, all tied up with a pink ribbon. I aim to deliver them to the Big Barracuda and get my bread."

Jack, Merle and Loaf blinked in astonished admiration at Zodiac's performance. The silver-armoured figure considered for a moment before holstering its weapon. Zodiac gave a huge sigh of relief. "It's lucky that you ran into me. As head of Security, I am able to take you straight to The Tyrant. I'm sure he will be impressed with you, Mr Bozo..."

"Ah ... that's Hobo, dude."

"Indeed. Other bounty hunters more –" the Security Chief paused briefly – "shall we say, experienced ... have failed in their attempts to capture these humans. You will be rewarded most generously. Follow me."

Zodiac waved his ray gun at the companions. "You heard what the cat said – follow this Security dude or I'll give you a blast with this vaporizing energy weapon type ray gun ... thingy."

"There's no need to go over the top," hissed Merle.

Zodiac matched step with Merle and bent down to whisper in her ear, "Sorry dudette, just getting into role." The "bounty hunter's" forehead was creased with puzzlement. "Strange though. That silver dude seems kinda familiar..."

As they followed the Security Chief, Loaf sidled up to Jack. "Do we make a run for it?" he asked, through gritted teeth

Jack shook his head. "No. We're being taken directly to The Tyrant. That's where we want to go. We follow."

Shield Generator Room, The Dark Pyramid
"Leave the cat alone."

Slowly, the Kippans turned away from their petrified prey and stared open-mouthed at the creature that crouched behind them. As their terror reflexes kicked in, most changed into Rabbian Sleekit Cowrin' Timrous Beasties and cringed away from the apparition.

The KSS chief alone kept his nerve. Transforming into a Diamond-shelled Armadillo (the most heavily armoured creature in the known Galaxy, and certainly the most expensive) he faced down his adversary: his voice was barely shaking as he said, "What in the Galaxy are you supposed to be?"

"I'm not sure." The creature that had, moments before, been a mongrel dog, looked down at its horrendous body with approval. "I couldn't transform into any form I knew,

91

so I just made something up. There's some Dobermann in here, I know that much, plus a hint of rattlesnake, a soupçon of Sissilan Slashslayer and a side order of Eyeball-Popping Razor-Toothed Ear-Driller from the Planet Aaaaaargh! What d'you think of the needle-sharp venomous spines?"

"Very impressive," said the KSS chief nervously.

"And the horrendously long sickle-shaped claws – you like those?"

"One of your very best features." The shape-shifter began to back away.

"The teeth? A shade too flamboyant?"

"Just right – all three hundred of them."

"I'm glad you approve," said Bitz cheerfully, "because you and your associates are going to be finding out just how effective they are if you're still hanging around three seconds from now..."

Two and a half seconds later, the shield generator room was completely empty of hostile chameleoids.

"You OK?" asked Bitz.

"Wuuurrrggghhh..." The paralysis induced by the Vampire-Skunks was already wearing off. Googie found she could move her legs again, though she had to think about it. Her voice shook a little as she said, "Thanks, dogbreath."

"Don't mention it, fleabag." The creature formerly known as Bitz gave a grin that nearly paralysed Googie all over again. "Let's shut down the shield generator before something else happens."

But Googie was staring past one of his six ears. "I don't want to worry you, but something else *has* happened."

"That's a very nasty life form," said a rasping voice from behind Bitz. "Is it impervious to bolts from a plasma weapon?"

Bitz groaned. "I don't think so."

"Then put your hands up."

"I don't *have* hands. Talons, tentacles, take your pick."

"Put them all up and come with us." Defeated, Bitz reverted to dog form and turned to glare at the Vrug-Haka guard who, backed up by a full platoon of its fellows, was beckoning suggestively with a fully charged energy weapon. "The Tyrant wants to see you."

The Dark Pyramid

The companions were marching through a vast domed hall. Hundreds of beings of every description bustled by, few taking any notice of the humans or their captors. On one of the walls a huge viewscreen showed the battle that was raging above the Pyramid. Cheers and shouts rang out as the crowds of FOEs celebrated the downing of another Bug ship. Jack's heart sank as he thought of the sacrifice the Bugs were making on his behalf.

"This way." The silver figure pointed towards a row of open doorways on the far side of the hall. Trying to ignore the cheering FOEs, Jack, Merle and Loaf made their way towards the openings. As they drew closer, these turned out to be doorways into empty shafts. Uncertainly, they stopped and stood waiting for further instructions.

Merle turned to face the Security Chief. "What next?" she asked.

As though in answer, the silver-suited figure gave her a push in the chest. The Server shot from her grasp and fell to the floor.

"No!" yelled Jack.

Screaming, arms flailing, Merle teetered on the edge of the drop and fell backwards into the shaft. The companions looked on in shock as Merle hung in the air for a timeless moment – and then shot out of sight, *upwards*.

Jack gave a sigh of relief and rushed to pick up The Server. "An anti-gravity lift," he said to Loaf. "Just like on planet Helios."

"You next." The Security Chief pointed at Loaf. "Or do you need a helping hand?"

Loaf complied.

As Zodiac followed Loaf into the lift, a nagging thought flickered through Jack's mind. On Helios the lifts had led them into a trap...

The Security Chief motioned Jack forward. He took a deep breath and, hoping that Googie and Bitz were near to delivering their part of the mission, stepped into the lift.

The companions emerged from the lift into an enormous metal cavern, its sides creased and crumpled so that the glittering walls looked like naked rock. Condensation dripped eerily around them, forming shallow pools through which they splashed.

As they reached the centre of the gigantic steel cave, a huge chasm opened out before them. It was spanned by a single thin metal bridge, which shimmered against the blackness of the yawning gulf below.

"The Bottomless Abyss of Unspeakable Oblivion," said the Head of Security. "Breathtaking, isn't it? And it certainly would be if you fell. Please be careful crossing. The Tyrant will be very unhappy if you perish miserably before he has the opportunity to do horrible things to you."

Zodiac stood at the edge of the terrifying drop. He gave a nervous glance down and reeled backwards. "Holy moley, dude! We gotta go over that? I'm scared of heights."

"I thought you were a fearless bounty hunter," said the Head of Security.

"Yeah, man, but this is my day off."

Jack gritted his teeth. With a tense whisper of, "Come on," he led the way onto the bridge and across the abyss. The others followed.

Hardly breathing, Jack inched forward. Every step of the way, he expected the slender walkway to tilt or open up and plunge them to their doom. He could hear Zodiac whimpering behind him and knew that the hippy was thinking the same.

He could hardly believe it when the sound of his footsteps changed, and he realized that he had reached solid ground on the other side of the gulf. Turning, he watched as the others completed the crossing, one by one, and stood for a moment beside a small communications console, silently celebrating their continuing survival.

The Security Chief tapped out a command on the console, and the section of bridge on the far side of the abyss slowly retracted into the cliff wall. "Just in case any of you feel like leaving prematurely." Their captor indicated a huge blast-proof door. "Let's see if The Tyrant is receiving visitors." A silver-gloved hand pressed a button. The chimes of a two-tone doorbell sounded faintly from the other side of the door.

"Yes?" A tinny voice crackled from a speaker set into the doorframe.

"Head of Security with some – er, unexpected ... visitors..."

"Enter." A buzzer sounded and the door began to slide open.

Merle, Loaf, Jack and Zodiac exchanged glances and stepped into a featureless chamber with curving walls. Before them stood an intricately carved screen. From the other side of this, soft music played and Jack was sure he could hear the tinkling of a fountain and birdsong.

"The Tyrant's Audience Chamber," said their guide.

Merle stood with her head on one side. "Listen!" The others held their breath. In a dreamy voice, Merle went on, "That sounds ... kinda nice."

Loaf shivered. "You're right, it does. And that is seriously creepy."

The friends gave a start as the door thumped shut behind them. An electronic hum filled the air. The screen parted in the centre, and opened to reveal a fabulously decorated room whose graceful curves were traced out in precious metals. Fountains played either side of an elaborately formed winged chair, which had its back towards them so that its occupant was invisible.

"Your Unspeakableness – the prisoners," announced The Head of Security.

"It's The Tyrant!" Loaf hissed to Zodiac. "It's our chance! You've got a gun – shoot him!"

Zodiac looked at the weapon in his hand with an expression of horror. "Hey, man, I ain't never shot anybody in the back – come to that, I ain't never shot anybody in the front..."

At that moment the chair swung round. The companions stared in shock. The figure sitting in the chair was bound and gagged, but there was no mistaking its identity.

"Tracer!"

The ex-surveillance chief's visor sparked red as he

realized who was standing before him. He tried unsuccessfully to speak and shook from side-to-side, clawing desperately at his plasma chains in a futile attempt to free himself.

"I don't get it," said Loaf. "He can't be The Tyrant. He's tied up. The Tyrant would be the guy who *did* the tying up."

"Unless somebody else got to The Tyrant already, and tied him up?" said Zodiac hopefully.

A rasping, hate-filled voice reverberated around the chamber. "Sadly for you, that is not the case."

There was a clamour of whirring and clattering as dozens of trapdoors in the walls slid open to reveal a multitude of deadly looking automatic weapons. The companions stared helplessly at the arsenal of weaponry trained on them. Jack wrapped his arms protectively around The Server. Tracer gave a low moan and slumped back helplessly into the chair.

The Head of Security drew an energy weapon. "Put your gun down, Mr Hobo."

"Don't," hissed Merle. "Make a stand."

"A guy can't make a stand with his legs shot off," replied Zodiac. He bent down carefully and placed the weapon on the floor before backing away, arms raised. The Head of Security aimed at Zodiac's pistol, and fired. The weapon glowed red and disintegrated.

Zodiac gulped. "That could've been me!"

"You *always* give in," said Merle through gritted teeth.

The space hippy shrugged. "At least I'm consistent."

Jack faced the silver-armoured figure. "You knew who we were – and you knew Zodiac wasn't really a bounty hunter. You must have met us before. So who are you?"

In reply, the Head of Security reached up and, with a dramatic sweeping movement, took off the helmet, to reveal a mop of spiky green hair.

"Tingkat! I knew I knew her!" moaned Zodiac.

Jack recovered from his second shock in as many minutes. "Are you The Tyrant?"

Tingkat gave an ironic smile. "Unfortunately not. I merely work for him. He gave me a job offer I found difficult to refuse – escorting you here. He wasn't certain you'd find the way on your own."

Merle snatched The Server from Jack and flipped open its lid. "Help – t-mail us out of here now!"

A sign appeared:

No SiGnAL – SoS cALLs onLy

"This is an SOS!" screamed Merle. "You can't get more SOS than this! Get out of there, Help, and get helping!"

Her cries were silenced as the gilded room shuddered. Without warning, the jewelled ceiling opened out like the iris of a gigantic camera, and the floor rose. Moments later, the invaders and their captor found themselves in a

vast space filled with monitors, screens and hi-tech hardware so complex and alien that Jack could only wonder
at its use. "The Tyrant's personal command and control
centre," explained Tingkat. "Don't touch."

With an ear-melting buzz of raw power, the room filled
with blinding white light. The companions shielded their
eyes and squinted into the dazzling brilliance.

The unseen voice that had spoken earlier hissed out of
the luminance. "Welcome, Jack Armstrong, Merle Stone
and Lothar Gelt…"

Zodiac gave a sigh of relief. "He hasn't mentioned me."

"…and Zodiac Hobo."

"Oh, maaannn."

"What pride you have," continued the voice. "To think
that you could try to outwit me! Your failure is complete.
Admittedly, you did not lead me to The Weaver; but now
that I have The Server, this is of no consequence."

"You haven't got The Server yet," shouted Jack, ripping
it from Merle's grasp and holding it up. "We had a deal.
This for my parents."

"You can't do that Jack!" protested Merle.

"I'm trying to give Googie and Bitz more time…" whispered Jack. He raised his voice and called out. "I want to
see my mum and dad."

A hollow laugh echoed around the chamber. "And so
you shall."

The blinding light faded to reveal sloping, triangular

walls and a control console, behind which stood a hooded figure flanked by two glowing force-field cages. Jack's mother and father were in one. In the other stood Googie, Bitz and the Bug.

"If you were relying on your friends to rescue you," said the voice, which they realized, came from the figure behind the control desk, "I'm afraid I have to disappoint you. I also have your ship secured in a hangar. There is no escape."

Loaf gave Jack a mock salute. "Nice goin' General, *Sir*!"

"You're The Tyrant." Merle's voice was expressionless.

"Evidently," said the hooded figure. "It would appear that I hold all the aces, and you have only –" The Tyrant gave a chuckle – "a Jack."

The Dark Lord of the Galaxy stepped towards them. "I've been looking forward to this day for some time – when I should see you all once again."

The friends exchanged puzzled glances. "What are you talking about?" demanded Jack. "We've never met you."

The Tyrant's voice was impassive. "But we have. Many years in the past or, to put it another way, just a few days ago." The Dark Lord pulled back his hood. He gazed mockingly at Loaf. "Surely *you* know who I am."

Loaf's face grew pale with shock. He felt his knees give way. "You…" he gasped.

The Tyrant turned to Merle. He stood towering above

her, his cold eyes taking in every detail of her face. When he spoke, his voice was filled with the hatred of a hundred years. *"You didn't come back for me."*

Merle felt the blood chill in her veins. She let out a breathless cry. *"Lothar?"*

8

Loaf gazed at the Dark Lord of the Galaxy in horrified disbelief. He took in the prosthetic right arm, the calliper-supported left leg, the segmented artificial right eye: the tubes and wires leading to the belt-hung life-support units, the greasy wisps of hair, the wrinkled, sagging skin. "Boy," he said in hushed tones, "did *you* ever let yourself go!"

The Tyrant gave no sign of having heard his alter ego. All his malevolent attention was concentrated on Merle. "You didn't come back for me," he repeated. "When you were captured by the Warlord, I risked my life breaking into his headquarters to find you!"

Zodiac tugged Jack's sleeve. "Hey man, when did that happen?"

Jack's eyes were focused on Merle. "Different reality. Tell you later."

"Yeah? Wild!"

The Tyrant's voice ground relentlessly on. "Then you dragged me back in time to that lousy hole-in-the-trees planet, and dumped me!" Spittle flecked the dry, cracked lips. "I came back for you, and you left me there to rot!"

"It wasn't my fault," said Merle weakly. She was staring at Lothar as though mesmerized with horror. "They wouldn't let me…"

"Let you?!" stormed The Tyrant. "Did the Warlord 'let' me into his stronghold? No! I smashed my way in there to help you, and you could have done the same for me, if you'd wanted. But you didn't. You left me stranded with those leaf-eaters! I couldn't speak the language or eat their food – I was an alien, a fugitive, with no way of getting back to my own reality! When I realized you weren't coming back, I swore that I would have my revenge on you, and the whole stinking reality you'd brought me to!"

"Are you telling us," said Loaf weakly, "that you set out to conquer the Galaxy because Miss Lousy Picker here gave you the brush-off?" He shook his head in wonder. "I hate to break this to you, buster, but she ain't worth it."

The Tyrant ignored the interruption. "Fortunately, on the forsaken planet where you abandoned me, I found beings whose minds were full of resentment, jealousy, and petty spite. Tyro Rhomer and his cronies. Crude bullies; whining, pathetic malcontents; but useful. I secretly led their half-baked Hard Fist revolution."

"You joined the Hard Fists? But they were just a bunch of thugs!" A chill swept through Jack's spine as he recalled that they had left Lothar with Selenity Dreeb, their friend on Vered II. "What happened to Selenity?"

The Tyrant's shrivelled lips curled into a sneer. "Dreeb, too, was useful – for a while. I allowed him to create the Outernet, so that I might ultimately control it. But the wretched creature betrayed me! He inconsiderately died before I could eliminate him." Jack groaned and clenched his fists, Merle gave a gasp of horror: even Loaf shook his head unhappily. "Then as soon as I moved to take over the Outernet and use it for my own purposes, I realized that Dreeb had secretly arranged for some being called The Weaver to prevent me!" The Dark Lord's wizened body shook with rage.

"Tough break," said Loaf unsympathetically. He gave Merle a scornful look, and hissed, "You had the hots for this bozo! I guess this is really bad time to remind you of that, which is why I'm doing it."

"I rose above that setback," continued The Tyrant. "I determined that I would root out and destroy The Weaver and the loathsome Friends wherever I found them. And there were compensations." The Tyrant approached the chair where Tracer still sat, bound and helpless. "It amused me that the creature who was, in my original time line, the all powerful Warlord, was in *this* reality a sightless wretch whom I recruited as my Chief of Surveillance, to use and torment at my will – until he attempted, in his infinitesimal way, to betray me."

"You wanted us to get rid of Tracer for you!" Merle's voice was filled with loathing. "You knew we'd think it was you in that chair."

"I thought it would be amusing to see what you would do," said The Tyrant carelessly. "You really do have an overdeveloped sense of fair play." He sighed. "Now, I shall just have to deal with him myself, after all. Dear, dear. A Dark Lord's work is never done." He swung to address the room at large. "But as for my enemies, all who defied me are finished! The Weaver, Friends..." The Tyrant gazed at Jack and each of his companions in turn. "You humans, and your treacherous accomplices. With The Server finally in my power, you have all lost, and I have won!"

Loaf turned on Jack and Merle, his expression a strange mixture of misery and triumph. "See?" He laughed unsteadily. "He's me! I always said I could have been someone, if only I'd gotten the breaks."

"You make me sick!" Merle flung all her misery at Loaf. "Who stranded Lothar on Vered, you or me?"

"Who snatched The Server and went and dragged the guy out of his own time line in the first place?" retorted Loaf. "Why do I always get the blame...?"

"It wasn't your fault," said Jack flatly, "or Merle's. Don't you get it?" Loaf and Merle stopped arguing to stare at him. Jack continued, "Merle *had* to go and fetch Lothar; she *had* to take him back to Vered; and Loaf *had* to strand him there, because if they hadn't, Lothar would never have become The Tyrant. That's what Janus could never tell us. We had to help create The Tyrant, because without him, this reality wouldn't exist!"

Merle and Loaf were thunderstruck. Even The Tyrant appeared momentarily at a loss. Then, the Dark Lord dismissed Jack's revelation with a wave of his hand. "It no longer matters. The Galaxy is mine. The Outernet can no longer stand against me. All my enemies shall be destroyed."

Loaf gave The Tyrant his most ingratiating grin. "Hey, look, I never knew you were you – I mean you were me – I mean, we were the same guy from different realities. If I had, I'd never have tried to stop you getting The Server, right? Listen…" Loaf's attitude moved from fawn to cringe to grovel in one practised movement. "There's no reason for us to be enemies, right? We're, like, from the same mould." Merle stared at Loaf with an expression of utter disgust. "We could be buddies, you and me. Whaddaya say? I mean, it's like, fate, y'know? Maybe – one day – we could rule the Galaxy together."

There was a moment's complete silence. Then the Dark Lord turned to Loaf. In a voice of ineffable scorn, he said, "Don't be ridiculous. I hate you."

"OK." Loaf shrugged, and rearranged his body into its habitual slouch. "It was worth a try. If you don't ask, you don't get."

The Tyrant turned to Jack. "The game is over. Give me The Server."

Jack wrapped his arms around the scuffed black case

and stared defiantly at The Tyrant. "Release my parents."
In their cage, his mother and father, clinging together,
watched their son's every move.

The Tyrant clicked his tongue in annoyance. "You are
hardly in a position to make demands." He turned to
Tingkat and gestured at the cage. "Shoot them." Tingkat
took aim.

"No!" Tingkat paused. Jack, moving like an automaton,
handed The Server to The Tyrant. At a gesture from the
Dark Lord, Tingkat lowered her weapon.

The Tyrant held the battered case of The Server with
something approaching reverence. "At last it is mine.
Now, no power in the Galaxy can stand against me!" The
Tyrant flicked a switch on his console – and Tracer's
bonds and gag disappeared. The ex-Chief of Surveillance
blinked, stretched and rubbed his arms. "Miserable
wretch," said The Tyrant, "I have a task for you. One last
chance for you to redeem yourself."

Tracer's voice was unsteady. "What is your deplorable
will?"

The Tyrant handed The Server to Tracer. "My best pro-
grammers tell me that it would take them several gala-
days to bypass all the blocks and firewalls protecting the
Friends settings in the inner core of this device, but that
you could complete the task in a matter of minutes. They
will be punished for their ineptitude. In the meantime, I
do not wish to wait. You will reconfigure this device to

accept commands only from the FOEs, and complete my domination of the Outernet."

"As Your Abominable Majesty wishes." Tracer heaved himself out of the chair and took The Server with a bow. He shuffled painfully to the control console, and began to connect The Server to the FOEs network of the Dark Pyramid.

The Tyrant's bloodshot eyes bulged as he watched his minion at work. His cracked lips trembled. Veins stood out on his mottled brow. "This is it!" he rasped. "My enemies have failed. The Weaver, whoever he or she may be, will soon be at my mercy! This is the moment of my supreme triumph!"

"Cue shrieks of demented laughter," said Loaf wearily. "Is this guy for real?"

At that moment, the light in the room changed from harsh white to flame red, and a clamour of alarms rang out. The Tyrant stepped quickly towards his control desk and flipped a switch. The holographic head of a worried-looking Vrug-Haka officer appeared above the controls.

"Can't I have a moment's peace to torment my miserable captives?" demanded The Tyrant. "What is the meaning of this interruption? Report!"

"Deepest apologies, O Gruesome One!" The officer sounded on the edge of hysteria. "We are under attack!"

"I know that, imbecile. The Bugs are no match for my fleet…"

"Not just the Bugs!" shrieked the officer, so far forgetting himself as to interrupt his master. "The Terror of the Cosmos is upon us!" The Dark Pyramid shook.

The Tyrant stared at his underling, his face livid with shock. "You cannot mean – *Wiggly-woo*?!"

The officer gave a terrified nod. With a snarl, The Tyrant broke the connection. His gnarled hands flew over the controls.

Merle gasped. The walls of the command centre turned transparent – and faded out. The humans stared around. Below them, four vast sloping walls stretched down an unguessable distance.

"We must be right at the top of the Pyramid," breathed Merle. "That's why the walls slope…"

"Forget that!" said Loaf. "Look up there!"

Merle and Jack did so – and gasped.

Between the impossibly high platform on which they stood and the seething clouds of dust that hid the Dark Pyramid from the Galaxy, the remnants of the Bug fleet fought on against the overwhelming forces of The Tyrant. But something else had joined the fray. Directly above their heads, the spinning maw of a wormhole wheeled against the dust clouds. And wreaking havoc among the FOEs fleet, maddened by its sudden expulsion from its aeons-old lair, was the Great White Worm.

The enraged creature spun and pounced with awful speed. FOEs vessels shattered between its terrible jaws.

Its writhing tail cut swathes through the defenders. Others of The Tyrant's ships collided, or smashed into the Pyramid itself in their panic-stricken attempts to evade their new and deadly assailant.

"Whoa!" Zodiac whistled. "That dude is real fast! And real wriggly! I told you we hadn't seen the last of this baby."

"Janus!" Merle gave a whoop of glee.

"What?" Loaf stared at her. "You figure he sent Wiggly-woo through here?"

"Who else?" Merle was positively dancing with excitement. "He must have fixed it from N-Space. That must have been his plan all along! We distract The Tyrant, and Janus sends the Big W in to trash his fleet, then the Bugs can get through, and then..."

"Silence!" The Tyrant gave a shriek of rage and frustration. "Shore batteries! Engage!"

"Too late, big guy!" taunted Loaf. "We've seen this worm in action, and believe me, it can survive anything you can do!"

From the slopes of the Pyramid below, gigantic hatches opened and enormous energy-cannons swung out. Their muzzles rotated upwards as their sights were trained on Wiggly-woo.

"Go on!" Loaf chortled. "Give it your best shot. I tell you, man, you can kiss your pyramid goodbye! Wormey's gonna getcha..."

The cannons fired. Jack and his friends cried out and shielded their eyes from the titanic blast of energy.

When they could see again, the companions once again gazed upwards.

Loaf's mouth hung open. "I stand corrected."

"I'm almost certain," said Merle in a low voice as they watched the smoking remnants of the Great White Worm falling slowly all around them, "that wasn't what Janus had in mind."

The walls reappeared. Their view of the space around the Dark Pyramid was cut off. The Tyrant stood behind his desk, once more in command. "So that was your precious Janus' master plan!" The Dark Lord cackled mercilessly, "The fool! As if even the Great White Worm were any match for my forces. And so the Friends' final card is played, and my victory is complete. Behold!"

Above him, the four triangular walls of the chamber were filled with a mosaic of screens, each showing the holographic head of an Outernet Assistant. The air was filled with a cacophony of voices as they reported in: "Formalhaut Server, standing by…", "Rigel Server, standing by…", "Kippo VI Server, standing by…" – until countless thousands of virtual faces stared down at The Tyrant, who threw back his head and laughed.

"See! The Server you sought to keep from me is now under my control. The whole of the Outernet – mine to command! My revenge is complete!"

A familiar voice said, *"Don't you believe it!"*

As all the occupants of The Tyrant's command centre watched in amazement, the screens began to go blank – at first one by one, then in tens; by the hundred, by the thousand...

And then, the screens came back to life. Every one showed a holographic face set in a familiar offensive leer.

Merle stared. *"Help*? Is that *you?"*

The multiple Helps winked at her, then addressed The Tyrant. *"Hey, Grandpa! You're lookin' pretty cheesy, do you know that? You don't have a hope of contacting any of your creepy Assistants, because all Servers Galaxy-wide are slaved to me. All your communications are down, not to mention the weapons, tactical and navigation systems on all your ships. Oh – and I control the Dark Pyramid network, too."*

The Tyrant, wide-eyed, dived for his control console and punched frantically at keys. Nothing happened.

"You're wasting your time," said Help cheerfully. *"I'm in charge of the whole Outernet, which is a big responsibility, let me tell you – in fact, I'm feeling kinda pooped, I think I'll take a little nap."*

"You will obey me!" The Tyrant was practically foaming at the mouth. "You will..."

"Oh yeah? Nuts to you, buddy. Kludge off!" Help blew a resounding electronic raspberry, and disappeared from the screens.

The Tyrant pointed a quivering finger at Tracer. "This is your doing!"

"I'm afraid so." Tracer's face bore a faint smile. "You ordered me to bring this Server into line with all the others: but while you were distracted by the attack of the White Worm, I reversed the process. All the other Servers have been configured to this one. Therefore, from this moment, the Friends have total control of the Outernet."

Ignoring the delighted exclamations of Jack and Merle, The Tyrant whispered, "But why have you done this? How is it possible?"

"The answer to both questions," said Tracer calmly, "is the same. I am The Weaver."

There was a moment's stunned silence. Jack felt as if his brain were floating in zero-G. Tracer had been one of the top operatives in the Forces of Evil. He was their enemy! He had harried them from one end of the Galaxy to the other. How could he possibly be The Weaver?

As if he had read Jack's thoughts, The Tyrant cried, "You? The Weaver? Impossible!"

"Not at all," said Tracer quietly. "What better place for The Weaver than at the very heart of the enemy's surveillance operations? Where else could I have learned so much about what the FOEs were up to?" Tracer gave a rueful chuckle. "The Friends too, come to that."

"Spy," howled The Tyrant. "Renegade. Deceiver."

"You mean…" Merle shook her head in astonishment and began again. "You mean, all the time you were supposedly working for The Tyrant, you were really guarding the Outernet?"

Tracer nodded. "Of course, I couldn't stop as many of his schemes as I would have liked without arousing suspicion. But I stopped as many as I could …

more than you'd think."

"You shall suffer for this!" The Tyrant turned to Tingkat and pointed a trembling finger at Tracer. "Shoot this creature!"

Tingkat looked at the Dark Lord thoughtfully. "I don't think so. You haven't paid me. And your enemies seem to have the upper hand."

The Tyrant stepped menacingly towards Tingkat. Suddenly the bounty hunter's weapon was pointing menacingly at the Dark Lord. "I think I'd like to hear what Tracer has to say."

The Tyrant backed off.

Loaf was still staring at Tracer in disbelief. "You can't be The Weaver," he protested. "You kept chasing us. You were always on our case."

"But I never caught you. None of the FOEs did. Suspiciously inept, don't you think, for the most terrifying force in the Galaxy?" Tracer smiled gently. "The Friends were unable to prevent Server after Server from falling into FOEs hands: so when I heard that the last Server was on Earth, I made a plan."

"You wanted us to bring The Server to you," guessed Jack, "but you wanted The Tyrant to think you were getting it for him."

"That was part of my plan. But the only way of contacting all the other Servers simultaneously was from this control room: I could not use The Server while I remained at my post in Kazamblam. I arranged matters so that I'd be brought here by The Tyrant immediately after I had taken The Server from you. I made two attempts..."

"And we stopped you," groaned Merle. "Both times."

"Yes. The first time, in Tiresias' cavern on Helios ... and then at Stonehenge." He gave Jack a faint smile. "When you sent me here without The Server, I was afraid I had failed..."

"Why didn't you tell us?" demanded Jack.

"There was no time. Besides, would you have believed me?" Tracer's lips twitched. "On occasion, I'm afraid my FOEs act was a little too convincing."

Loaf gave a whistle. "You had me fooled." He turned to face the others. "Does anybody have any more confessions to make? Maybe we should get those guys out their cages and find out if they're really who we think they are?"

"The cages!" Jack cast an appalled glance towards the force cages where his companions, and his parents, were still imprisoned. He turned to The Tyrant. "Open them." The Dark Lord merely glowered at him.

"He no longer has the power to do that," said Tracer matter-of-factly. "The Server now controls all the functions of the Dark Pyramid."

"Right," said Jack hurriedly. "Help!"

Lines of text appeared on The Server's screen:

*I told you I was takiNg a Nap
wHat pArT of this diD yOu not
UndErstaNd?
klUdGe oFf!*

"Looks like Help's back to normal," said Loaf.

Jack rapped on The Server's casing. "Help! Lose the cages. Now!"

Help reappeared, wearing a nightcap with a tassel on the end. *"OK, OK!"* The hologram closed its eyes in concentration, and the force-cages disappeared.

Bitz raced around in circles, barking joyously. Googie padded across to Merle, arched her back and rubbed around her legs. Jack's father and mother rushed over to embrace him. After a few moments, Jack's father pulled away from the huddle and advanced menacingly on The Tyrant, rolling up his sleeves. "Right," he said, "I've got a bone to pick with you."

Jack stared at him, not sure whether to laugh or be horrified. "Dad, he's the Dark Lord of the Galaxy. You can't just punch him on the nose!"

"I don't see why not," said Jack's dad. "Anything that's got a nose can be punched on it. He's had it coming. Threatening you, upsetting your mother. Don't worry son, I'll take it on from here."

"Jack!" Merle tugged urgently at his sleeve. "He can't

just … I mean he hasn't a clue about what's going on."

"I know." Jack looked down at Help. "Listen, I want you to t-mail my mum and dad back to Earth."

His father spun round. "Now just a minute…"

At the same moment his mother cried "Jack!"

"Sorry Dad. Sorry Mum, you're best off out of all this. I'll be back soon, don't wait up." He turned to Help. "Now!"

Help sniffed. *What did your last servant die of?* But a moment later there was a blue-white flash of light and Jack's parents disappeared.

Merle gave Jack a sheepish grin. "Dads, hey?"

Jack grinned in return. Loaf muttered "Tell me about it."

He was interrupted by an animal cry of rage. Taking advantage of the distractions, The Tyrant leaped at the astonished Tingkat Bumbag, elbowed her viciously aside and snatched the energy pistol from her hand. With a howl of "Traitor!" he pointed it at Tracer and fired.

The Bug was the first to react. It lumbered across the room and hurled itself at The Tyrant. The impact of its charge sent the Dark Lord flying and Tingkat's weapon spinning from his hand. The bounty hunter made a dive for her pistol – but was brought up short by a pair of stringy arms, which wrapped around her from behind.

"Hey, man! Like wow!" Zodiac was beside himself with excitement. "I got the green babe! Wham, bam, not now, ma'am! Can you dig it?"

The Bug picked the gun up and stood towering over the prostrate figure of his former master. "Yes, I can, Mister Hobo. You are very brave – but I have the gun. I think you can let her go now."

"Oh – ah – sure thing, man." Zodiac hastily released the bear hug he had thrown around Tingkat, who regarded him with outraged loathing. The space hippy gave her a shamefaced grin. "Sorry about that, dudette. No hard feelings. Say, maybe one day, when this is all over, you'd like to take a little ride on Trigger? Whaddaya say...?"

"Jack!" Merle's voice was urgent. "Tracer's hurt."

The room fell silent. Jack joined Merle, Googie and Bitz beside the injured Tracer. "How is he?"

"Not good." Merle bit her lip. "We should find a medic or something."

"Too late, I'm afraid." Tracer's voice was a painful wheeze. "Don't worry – everything has worked out in the end." He gave Jack a feeble wink. "That's ... all ... folks..."

Tracer's visor went dark. He did not speak again.

Loaf's voice was unsteady. "Is he...?"

"I think so." Merle looked helplessly at Tracer's six arms. "I'd check his pulse, if I knew where to start."

Bitz threw back his head and howled.

The Tyrant gave a malevolent cackle. "So much for your precious Weaver."

The Bug eyed the gloating figure with remorseless hatred. "I think you have done enough harm." It deliberately aimed the energy pistol. Its clumsy fingers tightened on the trigger.

There was a blinding flash of flight and a deafening screech of electronic interference. The Bug paused as the screens above its head began to flash on again – but this time, instead of showing Help's virtual image endlessly repeated, on each triangular wall a multi-screen mosaic of a friendly-looking, beaked face formed.

Jack gawped. "Selenity, is that you?"

"Hi, Jack!" The young Veredian waved enthusiastically with all four hands and winked broadly at his astonished audience. "Long time no see."

Zodiac gawped at Selenity. "Do you know this … whatever it is?"

"Oh, sure," said Loaf weakly. "We go way back."

"A hundred years, to be precise," said Googie.

Jack was still staring at the screens in disbelief. "The Tyrant said you were dead."

"Only in a manner of speaking," said Selenity cheerfully. "If you look at it another way, I've been here all the time. By the way, my sensors indicate that the bounty hunter is making a getaway…"

"Tingkat!" cried Merle. "She must have slipped out while we were looking after Tracer…"

"We've got the head honcho," said Loaf. "Who cares about the small fry?" He pointed accusingly at one of Selenity's images. "Don't change the subject. Suppose you tell us just exactly what is going on around here?"

Selenity grinned. "Well, once I realized that your friend Lothar – hi there!" Selenity waved to The Tyrant, who stared at his image with sullen, stunned hatred. "When I found out he was helping the Hard Fists to take over Vered II, I began to make plans. I had to complete the creation of the Outernet, but I knew that as soon as I did, Lothar – he wasn't calling himself The Tyrant then – would have me bumped off.

"Luckily, while I was establishing the Galactic web, I met Tracer – a very brave and selfless being who offered me a chance to escape. His people are borderline telepaths who are capable of mind-melding with other life forms. Tracer was blind, and no other being wanted to meld with him. He offered me refuge in his own mind, if I could find a way to transfer my consciousness to him via the Outernet. It took me years, but eventually I discovered a way to do that. I guess you'd call it c-mail." Selenity gave an impish grin.

"Anyway, it worked. Back on Vered, Lothar's bully-boys found me slumped over my workstation and assumed I'd died from overwork. And I've been sharing Tracer's mind – and adding to his abilities with my own – ever since."

The pictures on the four walls above them changed: Selenity's beaky face morphed into the elephant-eared features of Tracer – but the visor was missing now. The virtual Tracer had given himself eyes, twinkling eyes that regarded Jack and the others with benign amusement.

"So you're Tracer," said Jack slowly, "and Selenity ... and The Weaver?"

The image of Tracer nodded. "All three."

"But where are you now?"

"Everywhere." Tracer/Selenity made a generous all-encompassing gesture with his six arms. "We prepared for this day long ago. We planned to project our joint consciousness into the Outernet itself, once it was free."

Merle rose to stand by Jack. "So now, The Weaver *is* the Outernet."

Tracer nodded. "Our consciousness exists across countless thousands of Servers, on countless thousands of worlds, throughout the whole Galaxy. It is almost impossible for it to be destroyed. The Weaver – and the Outernet – are safe at last."

Jack stared at The Server, which lay disregarded where Tracer had left it. "Then I guess we won."

Merle gave a chuckle of surprise. "Hey – I guess we did."

"Yeeeees! We are the champions! They line 'em up, we knock 'em down!" Loaf whooped and went into an elaborate touchdown celebration.

This was interrupted by a thunderclap of sound. The floor bucked beneath the companions, sending them tumbling. The walls blurred, debris fell and a choking cloud of dust filled the control room.

Loaf lay flat on the floor, arms clasped protectively over his head. *"What was that?"*

"A missile strike," said the Bug, "just below us. I dislike to speculate but I assume my fleet must have found the Pyramid's defences down, and begun its destruction."

"Hey, man – you mean they're, like, gonna, blow this place up?" Zodiac's horrified voice wheezed from the cloud. "With us in it?"

Coughing and gasping for air, Jack peered into the thinning dust cloud and called, "Merle … Googie … Bitz; are you OK?"

Googie gave a delicate cat-sneeze. "Never better," croaked Merle.

"Never mind about us." There was an edge of panic to Bitz's voice. "Where's The Tyrant?"

"Wait." Tracer's eyes were closed in concentration. A moment later they snapped open. "He used a secret escape route. Sensors indicate he's heading for the Audience Chamber – and he's taken The Server with him!"

"What are we waiting for?" howled Bitz. "Stop sittin' on your virtual hands and get us down there!"

Tracer nodded. "Right." Jack and his companions scrambled on to the section of floor that had risen to bring them to the Control Room. As the floor began to descend, Tracer continued, "I'm afraid there's another problem. Tingkat Bumbag just took off from

Airlock 7648, flying Zodiac's ship."

"She took Trigger?" Zodiac was aghast.

"Well," said Googie innocently, "you did offer her a ride."

"Yeah, dude, but I kinda had the idea that I'd be there with her." Zodiac shook his head sorrowfully. "Bummer!"

"You could say that." Tracer/Selenity's voice was bleak. "The FOEs are using all available ships to evacuate the Dark Pyramid. The Server will soon be your only way out of here. You have to find The Tyrant..." The voice was cut off as the ceiling closed above their heads once more.

Another explosion rocked the Dark Pyramid as the companions arrived in the Audience Chamber. Through clouds of dust and spray from damaged fountains, Jack caught a glimpse of a robed figure slipping through the heavy door on the other side of the room. "Follow him!"

The Bug lumbered in pursuit, but was quickly over-taken by the chameleoids. Googie and Bitz streaked through the doorway and out of sight. A moment later, there was a furious outbreak of growling and cater-wauling. By the time Jack and the others emerged into the cavern above the Bottomless Abyss of Unspeakable Oblivion, The Tyrant (the hem of his robes hanging in shreds) was retreating from the control console onto the nearer half of the bridge across the abyss. He had evidently activated the controls that operated the bridge, for the other half was extending from the cliff wall opposite. Bitz (with raised hackles) and Googie (with bushed tail) were stalking The Tyrant, growling deep in their throats, as he backed away to the edge of the bridge that hung over the middle of the terrible drop.

The Bug raised its energy weapon. The Tyrant laughed, and held The Server out in front of him like a shield. "You dare not shoot. You risk destroying this." Glowering, the Bug lowered the pistol.

"We have to stop him before he gets to the anti-gravity lifts," said Jack as the floor rocked once again. "If he escapes into the Pyramid, we'll never find him: he'll get clean away."

Merle stood over the control console tapping frantically at keys. "He must have used a manual control to activate the bridge," she wailed, "but it's no good, I can't find it..."

The Bug reached across in front of her and slammed down one huge ham-like fist. The control panel shattered: sparks and smoke poured out. The bridge stopped. The Bug turned to Merle and said, very seriously, "Impact technology."

Merle stared back at it. "Impact technology?"

"Yes – if you can't make it work, hit it."

Merle looked at the smoking remains of the bridge controls. "I'll bear that in mind." The sound of another explosion ripped through the cavern. Cracks appeared in the metal walls.

Jack strode to the end of the bridge and called to The Tyrant. "Lothar – give yourself up. Having The Server isn't going to do you any good now. You'll never get control of the Outernet back from the Friends'."

"Perhaps not." The Tyrant took his eyes off Googie and Bitz for long enough to check that the gap between bridge sections was too wide for him to jump. When he turned back to face Jack, his voice was cold and harsh. "But The Server has other functions." The Dark Lord tapped at The Server's keys.

Ching! Help appeared. *"Hey, ugly! What's on your mind?"*

The Tyrant glowered at the hologram. "Prepare to t-mail, you misbegotten machine."

Help turned the back of its head towards the Dark Lord. *"Shan't!"*

"Then I shall input the commands manually." The Tyrant continued to tap at the keyboard.

"Help!" cried Merle. "Don't let him get away! Shut down your t-mail function!"

"If you do," warned The Tyrant, "I will drop you into the abyss."

Help gulped. *"Hey, my self-preservation chip has suddenly come back on line. t-mail enabled."*

The Dark Lord's finger hovered over the "Send" key. "I believe the usual salutation in these circumstances is, 'So long, suckers'!"

Then, everything happened at once.

As The Tyrant's finger descended on the "Send" key, Googie and Bitz, snarling viciously, darted at his ankles. The Tyrant shrieked with pain and rage, and The Server spun from his grasp and clattered to the floor. A swirling vortex of blue-white light appeared.

Zodiac shielded his eyes. "What happened?"

"Bitz and Googie interrupted the transmission," whispered Merle. "They created a t-mail event with no destination."

"But what *is* that thing?"

"A portal, like the one that sent Janus into N-Space. A gateway to oblivion."

Even as Merle spoke, the Bug lumbered into a charge. It pounded on to the bridge, which shuddered under its weight, and hurled itself upon The Tyrant. With astonishing speed, the Dark Lord dropped to the deck of the bridge. Unable to stop, the Bug soared over the prostrate figure, hit the vortex in its centre, passed straight through – and disappeared.

The Tyrant staggered to his feet, laughing insanely. "So perish all my enemies!" he howled. "Do what you will … I shall prevail!"

Fists clenched, Jack and Merle stepped on to the bridge and walked slowly but resolutely towards the Dark Lord. After a moment's hesitation, Zodiac and Loaf followed.

The Tyrant gave them a dreadful smile. "Farewell, my dear Friends. It is time for me to complete my escape. Enjoy your victory while you can, for this I promise you; one day, I shall return." He stooped to retrieve The Server.

At that moment, and before anyone could make a move, the vortex behind The Tyrant flickered. The Bug's huge hand broke through its swirling surface like a swimmer's thrusting up from water. It closed round The Tyrant's neck, and heaved. With a terrible shriek of rage and a final despairing cry of "I shall return!" the Dark Lord was dragged backwards into the vortex…

…and disappeared.

A tremendous explosion seemed to rock the Dark Pyramid to its foundations. The bridge began to tilt.

Jack gazed around him. Everything seemed to be happening in slow motion. The bridge was tilting further. Zodiac, Loaf and Merle were on all fours, trying to hold on. Bitz and Googie scrabbled frantically at the bridge's smooth surface. The Server slid, spinning, towards the edge…

"Help!" cried Help. *"And I don't need to be told how ironic that sounds!"*

"Do something!" screamed Merle. With a desperate cry, Jack made a dive for The Server. His fingers grabbed at the scarred casing just as the bridge gave way. Screaming, the companions hurtled headlong into the abyss.

10

"Aaaaaaaaaaaaaaarrrrrrrrrrgggggggggghhhhhhhh!" screamed Jack. Googie overtook him, tumbling slowly, legs flailing hopelessly at nothing.

Ching! Help popped into existence, hovering as usual above the keyboard of The Server. *"Going down!"* the hologram remarked cheerfully.

Jack filled his lungs again. "Aaaaaaaaaaaaaaarrrrrrrrrrggggggggghhhhhhh!"

"It might interest you to know that the Bottomless Abyss isn't really bottomless," Help continued in conversational tones.

"Aaaaaaaaaaaaaaarrrrrrrrrrgggggggggghhhhhhhh!"

"Although it is, of course, very deep. At the bottom is a cold, dark ocean, swarming with Flesh-Ripping Piranha Squid from the planet…"

"Aaaaaaaaaaaaaaarrrrrrrrrrgggggggggghhhhhhhh!"

"No, no – 'Aaaaaargh!' Only six 'a's, though I guess, in the circumstances, we should make allowances," said Help smugly. *"The point is, it's a very long way to fall. And if, at some point during your descent, you'd care to t-mail*

somewhere else, you only have to let me know." Help began humming a little tune.

"Aaaaaaaaaaaa…" Jack broke off in mid-scream. T-mail – of course! He still had The Server. "Help! T-mail us out of here! All of us! Right now!"

"Sure thing," said Help. *"Where would you like to go?"*

"Anywhere! It doesn't matter! Do it!"

Help gave Jack an outrageous wink. "Your wish is my command. Coordinates set."

Jack scrabbled at The Server's keys, desperately trying to hit the "Send" button. He felt himself slipping into unconsciousness … and then there was a flash of brilliant blue-white light, and Jack felt his body being torn apart.

N-Space

For a moment, Jack wondered if the t-mail had failed. Was he dead? Then the light changed form, becoming a part-icle stream of ever-changing colours. Jack realized that he was in a leaf-lined room, filled with cylindrical computers and screens perched on wooden benches. This was Selenity's tree-house, which they had visited in another time: the place where The Outernet had begun.

"I'm back in N-Space, aren't I?" said Jack aloud. "This is from my memory."

"And from others' memories." Jack spun round swiftly. Janus stood watching him, a slight smile creasing his cat-eyed face. Tracer sat on one side of him, Selenity on the other. "Welcome."

A wave of panic coursed through Jack. "Where are the others?"

Selenity grinned. "Do not worry, they are safe. With the cooperation of The Server, we teleported them back to Earth. I wanted our meeting here to be a private one."

Jack looked from one familiar alien face to the others. "How long have you been working together?"

Tracer gave a rueful chuckle. "Not for long. Selenity and I weren't even aware of Janus until after you'd defeated us on Helios – and even since then, most of the time our contact was intermittent and confusing, and we ended up working at cross-purposes. We only established full contact when I … died, and my consciousness entered the Outernet."

Jack was silent for a moment. Then he turned to Janus and said, "Did you know everything was going to work out like this?"

Janus' gaze was steady, and his voice was sombre. "I am sorry I was not more open with you." He sighed. "It is often the way that the greatest deeds are done by those who have least idea that they are doing them."

"You used me," said Jack without accusation. It was merely a statement of fact. "You used all of us."

Janus' voice held no apology. "Yes – I used you to take The Server back in time, and give Selenity the information he needed to start the Outernet; Merle to bring Lothar from an alternative time line to your own reality, Loaf to leave him on Vered II. I even used Lothar himself, and manipulated him to become The Tyrant."

Jack looked Janus straight in the eyes. "Why?"

"You would not ask if you had seen what the Galaxy was like without The Tyrant – as Merle did when she visited Lothar's timeline. The Galaxy was hopelessly divided. Warlords fought in endless petty conflicts. In that time line there was starvation, confusion, anarchy, endless misery."

"Because they *didn't* have a Tyrant?" Jack stared at Janus in confusion.

"Yes. But in this time line, opposition to The Tyrant united the squabbling worlds. They used Selenity Dreeb's creation to communicate with each other. Thus the Outernet spread throughout the Galaxy."

"Then without The Tyrant," said Jack, "there wouldn't be an Outernet?"

"Exactly." Janus sighed. "Therefore, I had to ensure that The Tyrant came into being. But in N-Space I had no physical reality. I had to work through others. And, as my Friend Tracer says, I did not discover The Weaver's true identity until it was almost too late. But somehow, together, we seem to have stumbled upon a solution. The Tyrant's power is gone; and now, together, Tracer, Selenity and I can protect the Outernet."

Another thought struck Jack. "And what about Lothar – I mean The Tyrant? Is he dead or will he return?"

Janus shook his head. "I cannot say. I have not sensed his arrival in N-Space. I have no idea where the vortex may have taken him. That is why we must remain vigilant, and why we have brought you here."

Selenity smiled. "At the start of your adventure, in some way we may never understand, The Server chose you. It was a good choice. And when you leave here to return to the universe of time, dimension and matter, it is time for you to take on the title of The Weaver."

"Me – The Weaver!" exclaimed Jack with a mixture of shock and horror. "I thought *you* were going to protect the Outernet."

"We shall, but we have no physical form," replied Selenity. "The beings of the Galaxy need to know that there is someone called The Weaver who will help to preserve them from harm."

"But why me?" said Jack, helplessly. "I don't know any-thing about anything! I just want to go back home."

"Do not worry, you will," reassured Janus. "Look on your appointment as an apprenticeship. Selenity, Tracer and I will watch over you from N-Space."

Selenity smiled at Jack, but his voice was sombre. "There may come a time when you will need to act again in defence of the Outernet. I am not sure that we have seen the last of The Tyrant."

"And what about The Server?" said Jack. "If the Outernet is in the hands of the Friends, will they need it any more?"

Tracer shook his head. "We have agreed that it should remain independent of the Outernet. We must have insurance against anyone attempting to take over the Galactic Web. The Server will be that insurance."

"So what happens to it?" said Jack.

Janus told him. "And now it is time to return," he concluded. "Your parents and friends are waiting." Janus' cat-eyes flashed as he smiled. "You have done well. Thank you, Jack Armstrong."

Selenity and Tracer joined Janus in making the secret sign of the Friends.

"Go well, Weaver."

And as the whirlpool of blue-white light wrapped around him, Jack knew that this time he really was going home.

USAF Base, Little Slaughter, near Cambridge, England Two months later

Jack, Merle and Loaf stood in the grey, cold departure hall looking out at the cumbersome transport aircraft standing on the runway. Master Sergeant Gelt, Loaf's father, was already on board, ready for the trip home across what Loaf insisted on referring to as "the Pond". At Merle's request (or more precisely, insistence) her father, Colonel Stone, had allowed Jack on to the air base to say good-bye to her and Loaf. The colonel was busy doing handover stuff with his successor, giving his daughter,

Jack and Loaf the opportunity to have a few minutes together on their own.

"It looks like we're all moving on," said Merle.

"To bigger and better things," enthused Loaf.

"Maybe." Jack glanced at Merle, who returned a wistful smile.

"Well, my old man's got a new job," said Loaf. "So has the colonel, and so has yours, Jack. Like I say – better all round."

Before Jack could disagree, Merle cut in. "When do you move to the new farm?"

"In a couple of weeks," replied Jack. "Dad's looking forward to it. He's a different person. Of course, it won't be like having our own place. Dad's only going to be the manager."

"For a company called *Friendly Organics*, right?" Merle gave a laugh. "Good name. Appropriate!"

Jack glanced outside as the engines of the plane roared into life.

"Shame you don't have The Server any more," said Loaf. "America would have been just a quick t-mail away."

Merle caught Jack's eye. He gave a non-committal shrug.

"This flight is going to be so booooring," moaned Loaf. "Air force food as well." He held up a carrier bag crammed full of doughnuts, biscuits and crisps. "Had to prepare my own light snackette for the journey." He glanced down at the stereo Walkman that Jack was holding. "That's what I need – some entertainment. There's no movie or music on those birds."

Jack gave him an uncomfortable grin. "Hands off. Buy your own."

Loaf gave a snort. "Doesn't look much good anyway – my old man could have sold you a better one than that piece of junk."

"I'm happy with it," said Jack, slipping the portable CD player in his coat pocket as Merle gave him a knowing look.

"Shame Googie and Bitz couldn't be here," she said.

"They daren't risk coming on to the base – with your dad knowing that they're from other worlds. He'd have had them arrested on sight."

"I suppose so," agreed Merle. "Especially with his new job in Washington – he's not told me what it is, but I think it's to do with aliens and stuff like that."

"Well, I suppose it's all worked out in the end," said Jack.

"We saved the Galaxy from ultimate evil!" exclaimed Loaf. He gave a low whistle. "To think that there's another me out there somewhere – the most evil dude in the Galaxy. Amazing!"

"Not really," said Merle pointedly. "Hadn't you better get to the plane?"

Loaf looked puzzled. "Aren't you coming?"

Merle just stared at Loaf, motioning him doorwards.

The dime dropped.

"Oh riiiight," said Loaf. "You two have got to do some kinda slushy, kissy-kissy farewell scene which I do *not* want to see. I'm outta here. So long Jack – it's been … different."

Jack gave a wave as Loaf lumbered out of the door, listing noticeably to one side under the weight of his goodie bag. There was a pause as Merle and Jack faced each other.

"So…"

"So…"

Another pause.

"You heard from Zodiac?"

Merle nodded. "He e-mailed me. Says he's doing fine in California. Orange hair, green beard, duds straight out of 'Hair' – he's just part of the scenery."

The noise of the aircraft's engines grew louder.

Tears trickled down Merle's face. Angrily, she wiped at them with the back of her hand. "I swore I wouldn't do that. I'd better be going." Merle bit her lip. "You know you can come visit. Any time."

Jack patted his coat pocket. "I might do that."

Merle smiled and brushed at her damp cheek. "Keep in touch." Making the secret sign of Friendship, she leaned forward and kissed Jack. "Go well, Friend."

Jack felt his cheeks grow hot and tears spring to his

eyes. Blinking through a watery veil, he could hardly make out Merle's blurred figure as she stepped through the door and hurried across the tarmac to the waiting plane. He moved forward, and stood at the window watching the plane taxi out, turn, open up its engines, roar down the runway and lift into the darkening sky.

Jack stared after the steeply climbing plane as, for a moment, it was silhouetted against the shimmering disc of the full moon. Although the stars weren't yet visible, Jack knew they were there; and orbiting the stars, millions of planets, home to the countless billions of life forms linked together by the Outernet. Earth suddenly seemed very small.

"One day," he whispered, "we'll be out there, too. One day."

An orderly stepped into the room and held open the door. "That's it, kid. Time's up…"

Jack gave a deep sigh and glanced once more out of the window to see the flashing lights of the aircraft disappearing from sight. Then he turned and headed for home.

As Jack stepped out of the air base, he was joined by a blue-haired cat and a scruffy-looking dog. They padded along either side of him.

"Meowwwwww?"

"Woof, woof!"

"Just a minute," said Jack, reaching into his pocket and pulling out his Walkman. He slipped on the earpiece and pressed the ON button.

"I asked," said Googie, "was it a touching farewell?"

Bitz gave a yap of disapproval. "You know, even for a Kippan, you're one cold customer."

"It was OK," said Jack.

"Well, if you want cheering up," said Bitz. "And if I can be of any help…"

Ching! A familiar-looking hologram shot out from the Walkman. *"You never let me say goodbye! Parting could have been such sweet sorrow!"*

Jack held up the Walkman and addressed the hologram. "Only Merle knows I've still got The Server – I didn't want Loaf or Colonel Stone to find out about it."

"You're ashamed of me, admit it! Anyhow," grumbled Help, *"why do I have to be disguised as this electronic dinosaur?"*

"Because everyone on this planet has one. You'll never be noticed. And you'll get to play some great music."

"Music!" said Help scathingly, *"you want music? I'll give you music."* A screeching cacophony of wails erupted from the Walkman. *"Waaahhhh! Uuurrfffff! Nnnnnughhh! This is Denubian folk music – popular on Denubia, but nowhere else in the Galaxy. Nddddummm, vvvveeeeee-jjjjjj…"*

Jack thrust the Walkman in his pocket where its

"singing" became mercifully indistinct. "Have you decided what you're going to do?" he asked Googie.

The Chameleoid yawned. "I got an o-mail from a contact in the KSS. Now we're not being employed by the FOEs any more, I hear there's a bit of a financial crisis, and I'm being blamed for it. I guess I may as well stick around here – for a while."

"Yeah," said Bitz, "and I'm gonna stick around here with you – someone has to watch over you and The Server." He gave the cat a mischievous grin. "You know, Googie, this could be the start of a beautiful friendship…"

By the time they reached the village it was dark. The stars had come out. They hung in glittering skeins across the night sky, shining brightly in the clear country air – a reminder of all that had passed, a promise of all that was to come.

Once you've logged on to the Outernet, use this space to record your identification.

AGENT I.D. NUMBERS

PASSWORDS

Remember to write down your passwords in sequence – and enter your most recent password when you log on.

Friend or Foe?

Jack read the o-mail with a growing sense of unease. "The Tyrant? Online threats?" He gave the others a half-ashamed look. "Look, I've just had a really weird thought. Is this really a game? I mean we don't know what this thing is – it doesn't look like any laptop I've ever seen. And all that stuff about downloading information on Earth … I mean, we couldn't really be talking to aliens – could we?"

"Aliens? Little green men?" Loaf guffawed. "Phone home, Jack. The truth is out to lunch…"

Loaf's taunts were cut off by a creaking noise, like the opening of a door to some haunted castle. This was followed by a thin wail: a plaintive, forlorn, tormented sound; unearthly and completely inhuman.

Three heads turned slowly. Three pairs of eyes focused on the door to the room, which was slowly swinging open.

A blue-grey face with luminous, golden, slanting eyes edged round the door and stared expressionlessly at them.

"Meeoow."

Three pairs of lungs expelled air simultaneously. Merle reached down and stroked the cat's head. "Hi, Googie." She looked up, rather shamefaced. "I've got to remember to oil that cat-flap."

"I've never seen a cat that colour before," said Jack, admiring Googie's shimmering blue-grey fur.

"Yeah, she's from Thailand. There aren't many around. She's a Korat."

"I thought Korats were orange." Loaf eyed the cat with dislike. Googie gave him an inscrutable stare and rubbed her head against Merle's leg. Merle grinned at Loaf.

"Scared you pretty good, didn't she?"

"Your dumb cat did not scare me!"

"Well, she scared me," Jack admitted, "coming in like that right after we got that o-mail." He looked back at the screen.

"It's a hoax!" Loaf's voice was scornful.

"How's that then?" asked Jack.

"It's obviously some guy sitting in a room somewhere, having a big laugh with us!" Loaf replied, sneering. "Pendar! More likely, it's some kid called Dexter, living in Hicksville, Idaho, getting his kicks by sending weird messages across the net."

"It could be a girl," Merle pointed out.

"Whatever," said Loaf giving a dismissive wave of his hand. "I'm telling you, it's just a game."

"I guess." Merle turned her attention to Googie. "You want some milk, don't you?" She hauled herself from the chair and headed towards the kitchen. "Come on, Googie."

Googie ignored the invitation and sprang effortlessly on to the table. She sat on her hindquarters in front of the computer screen and watched the shifting patterns, batting at the icon or dialogue boxes.

Merle came back into the room with a saucer of milk. "Hey," she told Googie, "cut that out!" She batted the cat gently off the table and placed the saucer on the floor. "There you go."

Googie ignored the milk. She leaped back on to Merle's vacant chair and gazed at the keyboard.

"She seems to be more interested in the computer than food," said Jack. He gave a groan and glanced at his watch. "Food – oh no! I've got to get home! I promised Mum and Dad I'd be back. Mum's making me a special birthday meal."

Loaf snorted derisively. "Big deal. Be fashionably late."

"Sure," agreed Merle brightly. "They won't mind, will they? It's your birthday."

Jack shook his head unhappily. "My mum will worry. And you don't know my dad. I'm late already. He won't be pleased. But if I don't show up at all, he'll make my life miserable for weeks."

Merle gave a lopsided grin. "He sounds like a bit of a grouch."

Jack felt a hot flush of shame spreading through his body. "I'm not saying … he never used to be like this. He doesn't mean to be…" Jack gave an angry, helpless shrug and grabbed the laptop. He hit the power switch and snapped it shut.

"OK." Merle showed him to the door. "But see what else you can find out about that thing tonight. And call round before school tomorrow, all right? I'll meet you at the gate."

Jack was right. His homecoming was not a happy affair. His mother had fussed around him. Where had he been? Didn't he know she'd be worried? You never knew these days; you heard such dreadful things. His father, who was already sitting at the table to make the point that Jack was late, gave him an angry look.

"Sorry I'm late." Groaning inwardly, Jack washed his hands and sat down. His mother served up the dinner – steak, Jack's favourite. They hardly ever had steak in the house these days.

Jack's father eyed the small portion of meat on his plate. He looked at Jack, then prodded his steak with a knife. He gave a snort of disgust.

"Like old boot leather. Still, what can you expect when it's been waiting in the oven all this time for someone to turn up?"

Jack felt his insides knotting up with guilt. "I said I was sorry," he replied weakly.

"Sorry doesn't make it right."

"Well, never mind," said Jack's mother with desperate brightness. "He's here now. Let's enjoy it."

Jack and his parents chewed their way through supper in gloomy silence. While his parents drank their coffee, Jack washed the plates and then went to his room. For a long time he sat staring at the patterns on the wall made by light from the street lamp outside, shining through the thin curtains.

After a while, he opened his schoolbag, and took out the laptop. This time, he had no difficulty in opening the case. The screen glowed. Jack connected to the Outernet, and logged on.

He ran his hands over the casing. What was this device? What did all the strange information on this site mean? Was it genuine, or was Loaf right? Was it all just some weird role-play game? Merle was expecting him to have tried to find out what else the laptop did, and he didn't want to disappoint Merle.

Jack sighed. "I need help."

In the blinking of a cursor, a blast of static burst from the computer. It was followed by a shimmering white light that hovered above the keyboard like a small cloud. In the midst of the cloud was a holographic, full 3D, metallic head. It bobbed around, eyes blinking.

"*Whadda ya want?*" rasped the hologram. Its floating

face had a sour, put-upon look.

Jack gawped in disbelief.

The hologram rolled its eyes in exasperation. *"Hello! Anybody home? Are you receiving me? And more to the point, whadda ya want?"*

Jack shut his mouth with a snap, reached towards the keyboard and began to type. W-h-a-t…

The head gave a whistle of annoyance. *"Don't bother typing. Just tell me what ya want, Brazza brain."*

Jack cleared his throat. "Right. Er … so you have voice recognition, do you?"

"I do," said the hologram snidely. *"Do you?"*

Jack blinked. "Well – er … what are you?" he asked self-consciously. He'd never spoken to a computer hologram before.

"Help, of course, you Munervian mindscaler!"

"What do you do?"

The hologram gave a pained expression. *"I've met some dumb species, but you… Gimme a break! I help: is that simple enough for ya? And if you don't need me, don't ring my bell!"* There was a small *"ching!"* and the hologram disappeared back into the computer.

A hologram with voice recognition! Jack was dumbfounded. This computer was beyond state-of-the-art! He grinned to himself. Loaf would go crazy when he found out his dad had given away a piece of hardware like this.

There was another *"ching!"* and Help reappeared. *"Oh, by the way, someone wants to see you. Beats me* why. You all packed?"

Jack stared at it. "Packed?"

"Doesn't your species pack to go on a trip?"

"I'm not going on a trip."

"That's all you know. t-mail initiating. Five ... four..." Jack looked round frantically. The walls of his bedroom seemed to be coruscating with blue-white light. "...Three ... two ... one ... t-mail is sending ... bon voyage, don't forget to write...!"

And then, Jack felt that every molecule in his body was being ripped apart. It was as if he'd been shoved in a liquidizer and made into soup. There was a timeless moment with stars; blackness, more light; then the process seemed to go into reverse, like a film played backwards, and the soup re-formed into Jack...

...who found himself crouching in a rocky tunnel lined with glowing tubes. A man was turning from a control panel with a look of startled horror on his face and asking:

"Who in the Galaxy are you?"

Jack gaped at him. "Who are you?"

The man put his head on one side and in tones of disbelief said, "Sirius?"

Jack backed away until he was pressed against the tunnel wall. "Who's Sirius?"

"You cannot be Sirius," said the man accusingly. Jack had a momentary vision of a tennis player shouting at an umpire. "Where is he?"

"I don't know!" wailed Jack. "I don't know who Sirius is!"

The man looked dismayed. He clenched his fists. "Sirius was supposed to be looking after The Server. I sent for him, and got you instead. What's happened to The Server?"

"What's a Server?"

"The device that sent you here."

"You mean my laptop?"

"What's a laptop?" The man clicked his fingers. "Never mind. I see what's happened. You're from Earth, right?"

Jack nodded. He hadn't a clue where he was or what was happening, but he was pretty sure about which planet he lived on.

"Then that's it. The Server has a morphic camouflage facility. It can disguise itself as an everyday item from whatever planet it happens to be on..."

Jack looked around wildly. "Look, I don't understand any of this. I was using my laptop computer..."

The man shook his head. "That was no laptop computer, that was The Server."

"You keep saying that. What's The Server?"

"Right now, it's the most important single device in the entire Galaxy. If the FOEs find out where it is..."

"Who are the FOEs?"

"Who are the...?" The man gave Jack a dumbfounded stare. Then he shook his head. "I keep forgetting, you're from Earth."

At that moment, Jack realized what was bothering him about the man's appearance. He looked perfectly normal at first glance. But when he stepped into the light, and Jack saw his eyes clearly…

The man's eyes were golden, with only a small rim of white. And the pupils weren't round. They were vertical slits, like a cat's. Jack tried to back away through solid rock.

"Who are you?" he breathed.

The man stared at him steadily. "My name is Janus."